CRUISING BACKWARDS

a novel by
KATHERINE BOWER

TATE PUBLISHING & Enterprises

Published by Tate Publishing & Enterprises, LLC
127 E. Trade Center Terrace | Mustang, Oklahoma 73064 USA
1.888.361.9473 | www.tatepublishing.com

Tate Publishing is committed to excellence in the publishing industry. The company reflects the philosophy established by the founders, based on Psalms 68:11,
"The Lord gave the word and great was the company of those who published it."

Book design copyright © 2008 by Tate Publishing, LLC. All rights reserved.
Cover design by Stephanie Woloszyn
Interior design by Janae J. Glass

Published in the United States of America

ISBN: 978-1-60462-972-9
1. Fiction:Romance   2. General
3. Fiction: Sea & Ocean

08.05.06

CRUISING BACKWARDS

This book is dedicated to my loving husband, Brian, who always believes in me;

To my wonderful family;

To Leanne, a true friend;

To my lost friend Thomas; and

To two wonderful teachers: Martha Clark and Billie Young.

Thank you all for your love and help.

ONE

Brianna stared morosely at the two tickets in front of her. They were all that was left of her job after today. She had started working at Smith's Law Firm about six months ago and had hopes of securing a stable position after the 90 day new employee date had passed. Instead rumors of a company buyout started to circulate. Now it had come to pass.

She had showed up to work as usual this morning and discovered a nicely packaged envelope on her desk. The first thought that crossed her mind was that someone liked to hand out Christmas cards early, it being the week before Thanksgiving. As she sat down to examine it further though the weight of it disturbed her. She slowly worked the glue loose around the edges and removed the contents. It all fell together:

Ms. James,

We have felt you were a wonderful addition to our group, but unfortunately as our company moves forward we don't feel that there will be room for you on our staff. It has truly been a pleasure for us to have you on the Smith Team and you will be sorely missed. Enclosed is a check for five hundred dollars severance and two tickets for a Caribbean cruise on us. As this is nearing the Christmas holidays we hope you enjoy this trip as a gift. Thanks again for your cooperation.

Best Regards and Merry Christmas,
Reginald Smith, Chief Executive Officer

Well, just great, she thought. What will I do now?

She pulled at her hair in annoyance, then gathered up her meager possessions and put them in a box. Once everything was together, including the check and tickets, she walked back to her car and headed back home. Her next thought was she hoped Ron had decided to go to work for a change. It being Tuesday made it kind of iffy, and a fifty-fifty percent chance that he'd be there. Lately, it was getting harder to put up with his laziness. With her job gone, she didn't have the escape she once had.

Ron Jones was like his name. Ordinary and dull. He was a nice guy at heart, but the nice hid behind so many other bad qualities. Driving down the road it was easy to think of such a list. Lazy was at the top. Conceited, dirty, and party boy were all descriptions that followed suit.

During high school or even while she was in college these things helped to lighten her usually serious nature, but now two years after she had graduated school and Ron was still the same.

He worked three to four days a week hanging sheetrock for a local contractor. It was a nasty job, but Ron liked it because he could light up his favorite type of Bob Marleystyle cigarette, put on some classic tunes, and zone out of his complicated problems.

His problem was his parents ignoring him as a child, while they were so caught up in the drama that is the Jones family.

Sam and Margy Jones were an odd couple. Married right out of high school in 1978, they decided to be groupies for a local Beatles tribute band, The Submarines. They followed the band around for about four months before Margy got tired of it and wanted to go back home to Suches, Georgia.

She said she wanted to open a store and sell clothes. Sam thought she had lost her mind, but decided for the moment he'd go along with it.

Sam had done some hard drugs while they were with the band on tour. Everyone told him it was going to expand his mind and let his spirit soar. He really liked that way of thinking. Soon he was all into the Free Love and No War scene. He started to not take baths and to spurn the Man.

That's the main reason Margy wanted to go home. She felt sure Sam was going crazy and needed to be home where things were simpler.

Things seemed to improve. Margy's store was doing okay. Until one day looking out the front window of the store a busload of anti-war hippies showed up looking for directions. Sam, of course, heard them from the back room where he was reading an interview with John Lennon in *Rolling Stone*. Sam liked Lennon. In fact he was one of his favorite dinner topics.

Margy was trying to explain which way headed toward Gainesville, and then Atlanta, when Sam interrupted and asked where exactly they were going.

"The Man's making a move! We're on the way to slow him down," said the hippie bus driver.

Sam jumped on this as intervention from above that he should go too.

Then Margy lost her cool.

"If you get on that bus, you better not come back thinking you're going to be welcome!"

Being in a righteous mood, Sam ignored her, thinking only of how to stop the Man once and for all.

Sam showed up about a year later. Shaggy in appearance, to say the least, and smelling of smoke, sweat, and sausages, his group had broken up days before. He'd not bathed in two weeks and had been living on a twelve-pack of polish sausages. Margy hugged him and then shoved him away.

She had worried and worried about him and here he shows up okay, but acting differently. More subdued. His eyes kept darting about like he expected someone to jump him.

First thing first, she made him take a bath and then fixed him some food. After he was settled, she asked him what had happened.

"It's over now. I don't want to talk about it, but we're moving tomorrow," he said.

"He's finally lost his marbles," she thought, staring at him.

She let the subject drop, sensing that it was too sensitive to talk about as of yet.

Later that night was thrilling and that's when Ron was conceived, because the next day they separated. Sam moved into the woods to live in a small cabin made of logs, with a thatched roof. He didn't have a phone or electricity installed. Those were ways the Man could find you. He dug a well and had an outhouse. Basically he was living the life of a hermit.

Margy continued with her store and tried to raise Ron up right. He went to his dad's on weekends and when he was old enough, his dad instilled in him the importance of herbs. Mainly marijuana. Sam grew the plant for his income. He did grow mint and some sage, but not for profit.

Ron always felt like he needed more attention. His mom was always tied up with the store and making him do chores. His father was always worrying about the Man finding his latest crop. His grades in school were passable—just good enough to graduate. Then he started his career in sheetrock installation. A friend of his told him he could work when he liked as long as the job got finished sometime. That suited Ron fine. Work a couple of days then party the money away.

Brianna had known of Ron from school, although he was four years older than her. They'd met at a party and hit it off. Brianna liked Ron's free spirit attitude at the time. So she knew all about his family and how he was.

Ron was a comfort zone.

No weird surprises.

She knew he only worked when he had to. Mainly when he needed beer money or his father had cut him off from his herbal supply and he needed a refill. He liked to watch

TV and eat at Taco Bell. His favorite show was *American Idol* because he liked to watch the losers act crazy, as he put it. For some reason Ron felt the world owed him and was around to amuse and entertain him. He lived off of Brianna's dime. It was her house and she paid the utilities.

Brianna had a fear of being alone and that's why she endured his pesky presence, or at least that's what she kept telling herself. She'd often thought of kicking him out, but as of yet, had not built up the gumption.

Thinking of the cruise she'd been given, she felt a jolt of excitement. She hadn't been on a trip since her parents died. They were killed in a head on collision with a cement truck. To this day she associated Martin Luther King Day with cement killers. She'd been seventeen when that happened, and felt so alone. It wasn't long after that she met Ron.

Maybe the cruise would be good for them, or maybe she could think of something to give her some direction in life. A new plan and a new start. Meanwhile she'd think positive thoughts and worry about what to pack. It was a seven-day cruise after all. A week would surely be enough time to come up with something and at least escape the damp December days to come.

As she stopped at the last red light before her turn, she glanced down at the seat where the tickets lay and talking to herself she said, December 28. Ship name: The *Enchantment*. Boarding at four o'clock in the afternoon. Port Miami. New Year's Party Cruise. Hmmm. What a way to start off the New Year. Floating miles away from home, where as far as the eye can see it's nothing but water. That's positive thinking.

When she arrived back home Ron's beat-up old Mazda was still in the driveway.

"So much for some private time," she murmured, while getting out of the car.

Ron was still in bed. On his days off he tended to stay in bed until noon, then raid the refrigerator for a late breakfast. She still had time to relax even if it was just a short while. Maybe she'd start a list of things to pack or sit down with her latest book. It was a romance about a woman lost in the desert searching for gold while being chased by an Indian war party. She was supposed to get captured and fall in love with the chief; finding out that riches weren't all life was about.

There is nothing like escaping reality in a good book.

As she started to pour herself some coffee, the pot still being warm from this morning, the door to the bedroom opened and out came the disgruntled leech, Ron.

"Thought I heard someone in here banging around. What are you doing home?"

"I got fired, Ron. Or I should say they let me go. The new setup they started with the other firm didn't include me."

"Don't expect me to pay your bills. I'm maxed out."

"Oh I wouldn't dream of burdening you, I know your expenses are overwhelming with that nice Mazda and all."

The Mazda was a 1986-style body with various colors of paint where someone had thought to attempt a camouflage motif. Dust from his many sheetrock endeavors coated the inside in a light flour film. Not to mention the many dents and dings from late-night beer-binge hunting escapades with his buddies and his spotlight named Roscoe. Notably the deer, or whatever they were chasing, usually heard them coming a mile away due to the bass speakers installed for their massaging enjoyment.

"Hey, don't be all crabby on me, 'cause you didn't seem important enough to keep down there. 'Sides, I need you to buy me some groceries. The kitchen's not got much in it."

"I'll go to the store later. Right now I'm making a packing list."

"Packing for what? You leaving?"

"No, Ron, they gave me tickets for a cruise as severance."

"Severance? What's that? You got some sort of disease or something? Don't tell me its crabs! Who you been seeing?"

Sighing and trying not to lose all her patience on his limited vocabulary she carefully explained severance.

"Oh," he said and then, "don't forget to pick up some bologna when you go to the store." As he went back into the haven that was their shared room, she sent a small prayer up for strength to make it at least until the cruise before she did something drastic like the song about the man, Earl.

She was just glad she didn't mention the five hundred dollar check that they gave her. Ron hadn't worked since Friday and with it being Tuesday she didn't want to risk him bumming money. Groceries were one thing.

About fifteen minutes later, Ron stuck his head around the bedroom door and asked, "I was just wondering. When do we leave?"

"The twenty-eighth of December in the afternoon from Miami."

"Well, that ain't too far away. Only a couple of weeks. Guess I'll have to call Jimmy and let him know. Don't want him missing me at work or anything."

She rolled her eyes knowing that he was just being the conceited jackass that was Ron.

When she thought of how her parents would have reacted to him, it made her blush.

"Bri, you could do so much better. Don't waste too much time on him. He won't change," she almost heard her father, voicing the words she'd said over and over in her mind.

"Keep your head up, honey," her mom would say. "You'll find the right guy one day."

If only they were still here so she could ask them for some advice or even just to have a nice chat. After five years the void of that loss still haunted her.

She picked up her book to try and think of other things, but other thoughts kept creeping in. If only she felt like she belonged. At least somewhere. If only she could find her niche in the mixed-up world. She really didn't have any good friends with whom to talk to. There were some people she'd known in college, but they weren't close anymore. Most had kids and their own families to tend. Maybe she'd meet someone on the cruise. Shoot, anyone would be an improvement over whom she was with now.

With that hopeful thought she soon settled in and was lost in the Wild West frontier created within the safe pages of her book.

TWO

The day of departure finally arrived. Standing in line at the port in Miami, Brianna and Ron eyeballed the other passengers waiting to board the ship, *Enchantment*.

"Looks like a cafeteria line at the old folks home."

"Hush, Ron, try to at least have at semblance of class."

"Sorry, but they're all over eighty."

"Next," said the clerk behind the counter.

Brianna handed her their boarding passes and stood patiently while the lady looked things over and stamped the appropriate boxes. Ron continued gawking like a frog trying to catch flies until he saw an even better example of his superiority.

"Bri, hey, Bri! Look over there. Yeah, that fat guy. Looks like he needs to go to a fat camp, not on a cruise. We'll have to get to the buffets early so we can get some food too!"

"Ron, do shut up. Please, people are looking."

"Oh you know they're thinking it too!"

"Oh hush!"

"Ma'am, you can board now."

The clerk, being fairly plump herself, glared at Ron.

"Honey, you could do so much better," she whispered.

With a smile of thanks to the clerk, Brianna eased Ron over toward the gangplank entry. While they took the customary photos for the people waiting to go onto the ship, she wondered if Ron must have been dropped as a child. How was she going to survive a week with that mouthy observationist? Surely he understood that his verbal diarrhea tended to offend and even embarrass people.

She glanced at their cabin keys to see what their number was. Isn't that ironic she thought. Room number 2666 was stated in bold print on the card. Kind of fitting, or a terrible premonition. Being in the company of her genial boyfriend it could go either way.

Settling into a cabin that should have been titled *closet* took some time. Although there seemed to be plenty of cabinets the walking area was jammed. When she finished putting away her things she noticed that Ron hadn't unpacked anything but his toothbrush.

"Aren't you going to unpack your things?"

"No, I don't want any weirdos going through my stuff. I plan on locking my suitcases whenever we leave the cabin. You never know what those foreign people like to mess with."

"Whatever makes you happy, Mr. Trust."

"I'm just cautious it's not about trust. Anyways, let's go take a look at this big boat."

"It's a ship, Ron."

"Same thing ain't it? It floats."

The ship itself had seen better days. The carpet was worn,

the chairs looked moldy, and the chandeliers were missing every third or fourth crystal. As Brianna noticed these cosmetic flaws, or at least she hoped they were just cosmetic, she was still determined to make the most of the vacation. She also saw that the other passengers were commenting on the ship's lack of polish. As they made their way to the elevator, she overheard two older ladies.

"Well, I asked the porter why everything was in such a state and you know what he told me?"

"No, what'd he say, Claudine?"

" He said 'Why would you want to invest in something that's just going to be torn apart in the spring.' Something else about a line in Italy wanting to gut the old girl."

"Sad isn't it."

Brianna had to agree with the ladies. It was sad to see such a large vessel brought so low.

"Reminds me of an old saloon hall," remarked Ron.

"At least the trip was free and we can enjoy the food and entertainment."

"Speaking of food. My stomach is running on empty. You think we can find one of those buffets?"

Although Ron was only five feet ten and one hundred eighty-five pounds, he could put some major food away. All the years he'd spent smoking pot and getting the munchies had paid off, and showed in his eating style. Normally, it turned her stomach to watch him gorge himself, but today with the ship leaving port she felt more alive and less likely to pay him any mind. Looking out the windows of the dining area and seeing the water churn as they departed seemed sooth-ing in some way. It was like she belonged at sea, on a ship bound for warm waters. Almost a sense of going home.

"Funny," she thought. "I've never been on a ship before, but it feels invigorating."

Noticing a glob of mayo clinging to his chin brought her back to reality.

"Wipe your chin, please," she croaked.

"Oh, sorry, must have slipped out of my sandwich. Want a bite?"

He held up the slimy concoction of turkey, mayo, pick-les, chips, onions, mustard, and beets. Yes, beets. Something about their pickled redness tickled his tongue's senses.

"I think I'm going to take a walk on the deck and watch us leave port. You go ahead an enjoy yourself." Who knew he could mess up a sandwich so well.

As she strolled the deck feeling the salt spray misting up from the turbulent waters her mind wandered. She had finished the western book and moved on to a swarthy tale of pirates and their unlucky victims. Gazing out across the vast ocean it was easy to picture the stealthy approach of a schooner as it stalked the slow merchant ship. It wouldn't have had a chance, especially on a dark night when the black hull would blend with the dark waves and the black sails wouldn't reflect moonlight. Sighing, she thought at least the book was exciting. So far this cruise looked to be pretty stan-dard and not eventful.

Later they met back at the pool bar. She had just ordered a Mai Tai when the band started to try and liven up the aging assemblage with some upbeat Caribbean music. She hated to admit it, but most of the crowd was fairly old. In fact she only saw a handful of people under 35. Most ranged from old to doddering. Still the night was young and the prospect of a nice pampered dinner that she didn't have to cook did sound appealing. Dress code was semi-formal for tonight so she shouldn't have to worry overmuch about her hair and makeup. Maybe she'd have another drink before getting ready.

Signaling the bartender that she'd like another, she decided to feel the beat of the drums and let go—at least for a while. Ron, having already discovered the bar after lunch, ordered his fourth beer and noticed a hot brunette standing on the other side of the pool. Considering that his ego exceeded his looks and that alcohol lended strength to his limited social skills, he was in his prime. Just because he was here with Brianna, didn't mean he couldn't have a little fun.

Meanwhile the hot brunette, named Shelly, smiled and started his way. He thought for sure that this was his shot at a steamy night.

Shelly saw Ron and thought he reminded her of an investor or some such eccentric money tycoon. His pants being Dockers and his shirt a nice pale blue Perry Ellis. She had no clue that Brianna had bought them for him so he would at least look nice until he opened his mouth. Shelly was with her current beau, a sixty-five-year-old retired golfer from Florida. He had retired from a real estate company in Key West, after selling mobile home lots in the 1970s. He was married, but enjoyed being a sugar daddy to sweet twenty-eight-year-old Shelly.

A new younger guy might be just the thing she needed

on this dull trip. Lord knew she didn't have anything to do while Petey, as she called him, was playing golf with his buddies on the upcoming port stops. She had planned to do some shopping, but maybe a fling with that nicely dressed guy would do the trick.

Brianna, engrossed in a daydream while watching the band, didn't notice the conversation that was about to take place. She was so used to Ron jabbering to anyone who would listen to his stories that it didn't register that he was considering cheating on her, even with her sitting right next to him at the bar.

"So what's your name handsome?" Shelly asked.

"Ron, sweetie and what's yours? I bet it's something pretty to match your eyes."

"Actually, no, it's Shelly, but you can call me whatever you like. So are you on this trip by yourself?"

"Uhhh, yes, business trip. Had to have a business party and thought 'Hey, why not on a cruise? It'll be good to get the boys on a vacation.'"

"Wow, that's really nice of you to take your business associates."

"Well, you know, it's nice to spread the love around," he said with a wink and continued to invent this new identity. It wouldn't be hard, he'd just charge anything he needed to the room. Brianna wouldn't argue, she was so easy going.

Glancing at her watch, Brianna saw that it was about four o'clock. Dinner was at six o'clock. If she went to the cabin now she could look over the itinerary and decide what she'd like to do tomorrow. Then on the way to dinner she could book any excursions at the desk in the lobby and go from there. Looking at Ron she saw him engrossed with a pretty brunette.

Good, she thought. Let her baby-sit him for a while.

She didn't really care if he showed for dinner or not. It was nice to have the freedom to breathe. He could be so suffocating at times with his look-at-me attitude. Besides, he had his own key, so if he needed anything he could use that. Not that she trusted him or anything, but surely he'd have enough sense not to do anything too stupid.

Easing the key into the slot on the door to the room she smiled to herself. One of the cleaning stewards from Thailand waved and said hello. It was nice to know that at least someone noticed her and liked what they saw.

As she entered the cabin she grabbed the itinerary packet off the nightstand and sat down on the bed to go over the choices:

Day	Port	Arrive	Depart
Sunday	Miami		5:00 p.m.
Monday	Nassau, Bahamas	7:00 a.m.	noon
Tuesday	At sea		
Wednesday	At sea New Year's Party		
Thursday	St. Lucia	9:00 a.m.	7:30 p.m.
Friday	Puerto Rico	9:00 a.m.	4:30 p.m.
Saturday	At sea		
Sunday	Miami	8:00 a.m.	

Scanning the pages, she noticed that tomorrow was Nassau and it sounded like a beautiful place. She'd seen pictures in some travel magazines and on TV, but she was to see it in person.

That's the best way, she thought. So she ought to do something outdoors. Let's see. Snorkeling, kayaking, dolphin encounters, what to do?

Reading the lists she finally narrowed it down to two choices:

Two-hour sightseeing tour.

> Visit romantic Nassau. Discover the ancient forts Fincastle & Charlotte, the Queen's Staircase, Government House, the Water Tower, and straw market. $25 per person.

Robinson Crusoe Cruise.

> Cruise the clear waters on our catamaran and then go snorkeling in the coral reefs and tidal pools. Eat, drink, and have fun. Wine & food are plentiful. Approx. $45 per person.

"I wonder if Ron will want to go. Probably not. He's not very outdoorsy," she said, deciding to do the catamaran cruise.

While she was getting ready for dinner she happened to wonder where Ron had gone off. Maybe she wouldn't be the one to find someone else. Maybe he would. She was thinking of the girl she had left him with at the bar. Of course Ron couldn't offer a girl like that much. She had that high maintenance look to her. Only money could support a girl like that, which he was definitely lacking.

"Ah well, who knows," she said, sighing as she shut the cabin door.

Dinner proved to be a delight even though she was seated with two obviously happy older couples. The first couple was from a small town in Great Britain and they'd been saving for months for the trip. It was their forty-fifth wedding anniversary and they wanted to do it in style. The other couple was from Louisiana and enjoyed food with relish. They owned a restaurant in New Orleans and had been together for thirty-seven years. They said that cruising was their favorite way to vacation.

The small talk roamed around grandchildren and some of their previous trips. Brianna tried to make polite conversation even though she didn't care what Bobby Sue who lived in Texas and was turning eight, had said. They were nice people who proved to her that the good relationships were out there. It was just a matter of finding them.

It was a little strange for her to be the odd woman out. She'd passed Ron in the hallway on the way to dine and he'd said that he'd met some cool people and was going to meet up with them at one of the bars. Cool people being: one Shelly with long legs that seem to go on forever. At the time she hadn't minded, but now sitting here with such close loving couples, it was hard not to let the loneliness creep in.

The food was divine, starting with escargot, followed by a crisp salad of baby spinach and pickled bell peppers. Her entrée was veal soaked in warm brown gravy sitting on top of fluffy smashed red potatoes with asparagus. Dessert was a light tiramisu. She always felt that food could be an art form. This meal was surely one of the best examples she had personally experienced.

After everything was cleared away, including the terrible loneliness, which she had banished to the back of her mind, she said goodnight to the others and decided to take a stroll under the stars on the sports deck.

Earlier when she'd taken her other walk the deck had been crowded with people playing shuffle board and toasting the ship's departure from port. Now it was soothingly quiet. Except for the few lovebirds gazing at each other with rapt attention, she was in her own world. A world of romance, dreams, and moon-glow. A place where she could imagine the man of her dreams. If only she could make him step out of there and into the real world.

Spying a twinkling star up above, she decided to cave into the silly whim of star wishing.

Not that anything will come of such notions, she thought out loud. But I might as well take the chance. I've nothing to lose and everything to gain.

Again the star seemed to wink and shimmer.

"Star light, star bright, first star I see tonight. I wish I may. I wish I might. Have this wish, I wish tonight. I wish— I wish I could meet the man that haunts me. That someone who could love me without me having to support him. He'd have his own strengths and courage. Something that seems to be lost nowadays," she recited.

A breeze seemed to be picking up.

"I guess I'll head back to the cabin," she said, noticing on her watch that it was already half past eleven and she knew she had to get up and be ready by eight o'clock to go on that tour tomorrow. Ron could fend for himself. She was going to have a great time even if she had to do it alone.

Thinking that he'd outsmarted Brianna by secretly meeting Shelly, Ron would have been galled to know that she'd had a better time without him. He pictured her reading one of her books, which he considered a total waste of time, wishing he were there. She'd been aggravating lately, but he needed her support right now. Hopefully that was going to change.

He intended to enjoy this trip to it's fullest. Not lounge around in the cabin wasting time on books. Between Shelly and the casino he didn't know how he could get bored. Not to mention all the bars.

He'd met up with Shelly at the Pelican Bar on the Lido Deck at seven p.m. She had dressed in a short red dress with sequins and a pair of black four-inch heels. She was in her element and that's just how she wanted to appear for this new tycoon.

Ron thought how lucky he was to have spotted her. Of course with his charm and charisma it was just a matter of time. He had dug around earlier in their conversation to find out Shelly's financial status. She'd quickly told him that she was on the cruise with her rich uncle. If only the old buzzard would croak and leave her all his money. Thinking this way made him wonder if he'd finally found his retirement plan.

Shelly on the other hand assumed a lot about Ron. She

figured he avoided money questions because being upper crust would not want to talk about it. To her that was all the sign she needed. Everyone knew that if you had money it showed and you didn't speak about it; it was just understood that it was there. She'd learned that from Petey.

Petey had told her before she left to meet a friend for dinner that he would be playing golf tomorrow with Waldo and Burt and that she could go shopping if she'd like. Maybe she could get Ron to take her and save the money Petey had given her for another time. She could always use some new things.

Their dinner that night included a hamburger followed by a round of body shots. After the fourth or fifth shot, considering they lost count, Shelly having matched Ron's body shots taken from between her breasts with equal shots taken on her own, they proceeded to make-out like two hyenas on a fresh zebra carcass. The bartender stared in fascination. He still swore he'd never understand Americans.

Finally after about fifteen minutes of carnivorous feasting he decided to break the two up and send them to their cabin. He didn't want his supervisor coming in and seeing this considering he'd already gotten in trouble for giving away shots to cute teenage girls.

As Ron and his high-heeled companion eased off their stools, he paid with his room key and they started their wobbly descent to the next bar. When they arrived to the other bar the door was just closing. They were getting ready to clean because it was nearing 1:30 and they had to be ready to open in the morning.

The two then concluded that their first date was ready to end or at least Shelly had. She didn't want to make Petey mad by not coming back to their suite and she still wanted to leave Ron hanging so he'd come back for more. Besides he was so slobbering drunk nothing could happen anyways.

So it was that Shelly helped him to his room. Even opened the door for him, not noticing a sleeping Brianna, as she gently shoved him through the door. Ron made about five or six steps before he passed out in a crumpled heap at the foot of the bed.

The thump noise that he made woke Brianna up and she quickly noted his drunken stupor and his sprawled body. She was just glad he didn't make it to the bed because he did slobber when he was drunk and she didn't want to be anywhere near one of his party puddles.

THREE

Shaking the sleep from her mind and contemplating the past couple of days. Brianna decided that her and Ron had come to an understanding. She would enjoy reading, the ship, and the new people while he partied with his new friends. Overall, it seemed to be working out nicely.

She had awakened early this morning, while he still wallowed in bed and would be there until almost lunch. Her goal was to stake claim on the perfect sunbathing chair. Learning early on that the process was first come, first serve, and that people were serious about their claims, she made it her mission to get comfortable before the battle over who could reserve which with what began. Discovering the perfect one over near the pool in the sun and in walking distance of the bar, she sat down and began arranging her things. Alternating between reading and putting on tanning oil she felt it was going to be a lovely day at sea.

As she took a break from the mysteries of her romantic buccaneer novel she observed many of the stragglers who'd waited until too late to stake their claim. They were trying to pull leftover chairs together, blocking the walkways with confusion and often misunderstandings. Squeezing them into small openings in hopes of sitting either with friends or their spouses and overall, causing smashed fingers and injured pride.

She watched closely to one such encounter nearby as some older men talked in a tight group near the pool. The men were obviously from a European country, wearing their unmistakable Speedo's and in dire need of back waxing. They were hogging the walkway and didn't look too inclined to share. Deep in conversation about the variances in the sharpness of cheddar, the group did not pay any attention to the approaching Yankees. Everyone could tell this combination had a good possibility of getting ugly.

With a characteristic New Jersey accent, the elderly man in bright red and yellow shorts that contrasted terribly with his white pasty skin said, " Excuse me sir, you're blocking the way and we would like to pass. Would you move over?"

"Oh pardon me, monsieur" one man said, and with a nonchalant shrug moved two inches to the left.

"You'll need to move more than that," said the pasty man scowling at the rude Frenchman.

The Frenchman, having been interrupted again from his fascinating discussion that had now moved to the aging processes of the above mentioned cheeses, glared disgustedly at the shorter man as if he were a fly and he were in dire need of a swatter to rid himself of such a nuisance.

Deciding that this scene was getting too dramatic for her taste, Brianna let her gaze wander to the rolling waves cresting upon the ocean. If only everyone could just get along and enjoy their trip. Knowing how futile that chance was, she eyed the vastness of the ocean. It sure was confounding how the horizon appeared so limitless. Everywhere you looked was water. Like the old saying, "Water, water, everywhere and not a drop to drink." Oh, how terrible it would be to be lost adrift without food or water. Floating along praying for rain so you could capture a few of the lifesaving droplets. Or even worse, to be becalmed without any hope of a breeze to move you across the surface.

"I wonder how sailors of old used to get by without going crazy when that happened," she pondered aloud.

Having already consumed a turkey on rye, some chips, and a delightful daiquiri, she sighed and decided it was time to flip over onto her stomach so she could keep an even tan going. It felt like it was the perfect time for a lunchtime nap. Something about basting in the bright sun made her sleepy. Maybe it was the glorious warmth of the sun or even the slow rocking of the ship, but either way a nap would be wonderful.

It looked to be the perfect day for luck or so Ron thought as he plodded beside a perky Shelly. With Brianna getting up so early it gave him plenty of time to woo his future investment. They were headed toward the casino and he hoped to show her how he was a real winner. Poker was on his mind. He'd already bragged about how he could just feel the next card. Like a sixth sense or something. Actually he'd seen the movie *Maverick* with Mel Gibson and he figured if Mel could have the power to change that important card then surely someone with his intelligence could too. He'd also been watching the poker tournaments on TV to pick up pointers. With those credentials he couldn't help but rack up some serious money.

He wasn't counting on a professional gambler like Sparky McPherson to be on board. Sparky didn't travel on the television circuit. He was a low-key man who liked the small-time bar scene. He'd sit at the bar and listen to the customers, all the while playing off the innocent old man bit. His talents weren't limited to poker however. He was also proficient at pool, darts, and could even drink the staunchest of college know-it-alls under the table. It paid off to be good at a variety of endeavors. You never knew which would bring in the most dough.

Sparky's appearance was average at best. He was around seventy years old, five feet ten, thin, almost lanky, and had dull brown hair. He preferred to be nondescript. As long as you didn't look him in the eye, which most people didn't when drinking, you wouldn't be able to tell that he was such a shark. He hid it well.

He'd won this cruise from a drunken sot in Myrtle Beach, South Carolina. The man was boo-hooing about having to take his mother-in-law to visit his recently deceased wife's grave in Florida. The cruise tickets had been reserved for the man and his new girlfriend. Discovering that the man didn't really need the tickets for anything more than a new fling, Sparky felt obligated to relieve him of the confusing choice. After a few games of pool, the man quietly relinquished his tickets and weaved slowly to the door. Sparky had won a nice vacation.

Sitting at the poker table in the colorful casino, he watched as a slim brunette on the arm of an obvious slime bag made their way slowly through the slot machines and turned in his direction.

"Good," he thought. "It'd be my pleasure to take that weasel down a few pegs."

Ron eased into the chair across from Sparky as Shelly gazed with hooded eyes at Ron.

"You go get him, Tiger," she said.

"Game's five-card draw, gentlemen," said the dealer as he started to cut the deck and shuffle.

Giving Shelly an encouraging look he settled in to show how good he was. Lucky for him he won the first four games. Sparky could read him like a book and the dumb oaf didn't know he was being set up. When he lost the next hand, Sparky leaned over and with an encouraging wink said, "Don't give up now, boy. I haven't seen anyone with your luck in years." Having the desired effect in inflating Ron's already huge ego, Sparky sat back with a satisfied smile and continued his losing streak.

Ron won the next few games and thought to himself that he could be in the tournaments on TV. By this time the betting had jumped considerably. Instead of the customary five and ten dollar range, the stakes were in the hundreds. Soon he had a large pile of the wonderfully colored chips in front of him. Glancing at Shelly, he could see she was impressed. When the bet rose to two thousand dollars he cockily pushed all his chips in thinking he had this one in the bag.

"Show your cards, please," the dealer said.

"A pair of aces, king high," Ron said, flipping his over with a flourish.

By now there was quite a crowd gathered around their table, clapping at Ron's good luck.

Then the dealer asked for Sparky's cards. Pretending indifference at the play he flipped them over.

"Three of a kind. Queens. Jack high," Sparky said, grinning from ear to ear.

"Maybe you can play again later, son. I'm going to go get me some grub. Nice playing with you," Sparky said.

Blinking in incomprehension, Ron just sat open-mouthed like a bass gasping for air.

"Why don't we go do some shopping now, honey?" Shelly said, not understanding his loss.

Trying to answer this new twist quickly, he remembered that Brianna had said the room key could be used for things besides drinks. Praying this was true he stood, taking Shelly by her extended hand and they walked casually down the hallway to the boutiques. All the while he was thinking how Brianna might kill him when she finds out.

Shelly had great taste. She loved jewelry and quickly spotted a diamond and opal necklace that she had to have. She steered Ron in that direction and asked the clerk if she could see it and then squealed in delight as the opal colors glistened invitingly with the diamond accents. Seeing her enjoyment made up his decision.

He purchased the necklace and then the matching earrings as a set for the low price of $1,748.95. The clerk assured him that he wouldn't be billed until the last day of the cruise, when he could just apply the amount to credit card or pay cash. By that time he hoped to have Shelly completely won over and it wouldn't matter. Brianna could do with the bill as she liked. His future was in the balance, after all.

Shelly had only just begun her shopping spree. Dragging a wary but willing Ron in tow, she proceeded to look at every store and vendor in the shopping part of the ship. By the time she had finished, she had accrued a new evening gown, stiletto heels, a delicate shrug, and a gold Bolivia watch to match the jewelry.

"What a wonderful New Year's gift," she gushed at Ron who was strutting like the head rooster in the barn.

With her new pretties tucked safely away in their appropriate packaging and Ron acting as the pack mule, she was feeling magnanimously towards him. So she asked if he might like her to give him a private fashion show of the new goodies later. Of course what guy would turn down a hint like that? Smiling smugly he agreed that it would be a great way to while away the afternoon. Who knows if afternoon will lead to evening and beyond? The only trick was to be in the cabin at a different time than Brianna. Was there something about today that was special? He couldn't remember, must not be too important then. Strolling down the passageway, he thought his luck from earlier might be turning around.

After awaking from her nap in time to apply some more sunscreen before she burned and realizing that she'd have to start her hair-curling process before long if she wanted to be ready in time for dinner she starting to pack up her stuff. She dreaded the long procedure. Being born with super straight hair, it would be a contest between her and the hairspray to keep the curls intact.

She wanted this New Year's to be special and she wanted

to dress accordingly. She'd bought a slinky black dress with black and blue iridescent beads. It was shorter than she was used to and had a low-cut bodice, but she figured she was due for something different and fun. She didn't know anyone here but Ron and the people she'd met at dinner. There was no one to point fingers at her like at home.

"I can't believe she's wearing that," someone would comment at one of those parties. Here she could let loose some and live a little.

Ron had only graced her with his presence once for dinner so far. He didn't like eating with the older couples. Their conversation bored him and his vulgar mouth caused plenty of silent lulls in the dinner banter. She could tell the others thought him lacking of sense and decorum. She had to agree. He was more suited for bars and sporting events. At least the drunks there could ignore him.

He was supposed to meet her tonight for a New Year's Eve dinner. She'd told him six o'clock sharp, but who knew if he'd been listening. Surely he wouldn't embarrass her that bad.

"Ah well, shouldn't worry about that right now," she mumbled leaving the chair for someone else to claim.

The curler was heating up and she'd laid her dress out. She felt jittery with anticipation. Trying to move around Ron's suitcases that littered the cabin she still couldn't understand his reasoning. She didn't think any of the ship's staff cared what a guy traveling in one of the smallest cabins carried in his luggage. It's not like this is the penthouse or even a suite. Back to the business at hand.

Contemplating her previous thoughts as she started rolling her hair on the iron she decided that one of her first resolutions would be to stop worrying about Ron so much and more about herself. She really needed to get her priorities straight and find someone who liked her for herself and not just a free ride.

Slowly her head started to sprout flowing blonde curls. If only they'd stay curly. Applying another coat of spray and doing the classic hair flip she then put on her dress, her shoes, and double-checked her makeup. Everything looked good; now for a before dinner cocktail.

Picking a seat near the window and sipping an Appletini she'd ordered, she noticed that she was turning some heads. All the work was paying off and it was nice to have people look. It made her feel kind of like a movie star or something. Catching a notably married couple near the bar staring she stifled a giggle as the wife elbowed the gawking husband. Winking at him before he turned, she decided the drink was making her goofy.

The ushers started herding the guests to their seats at exactly six. With her drink finished and a happy glow running through her veins she didn't miss her dining partner. She greeted each of the couples and they smiled in return. They all commented on how nice she looked and then asked about Ron. She replied that he must be running late, but should be along shortly.

As the evening wore on it became apparent to all that he wasn't coming. She tried to keep her chin up. It wouldn't be polite to let them see her obvious chagrin. She didn't want to bring them down with her gloom and couldn't stand to see the pity on their faces.

She'd ordered a bottle of wine in hopes of doing some toasts, but now she almost wanted to drink the whole bottle. Instead, after just a couple glasses she let the steward store the rest for the next night. The steward then came around the table having the guests sign for the wines they'd ordered. When he reached her he handed her a note along with the wine receipt. There was a problem with her room account. The note requested her to drop by the front office after dinner to confirm some information with them. Signing the receipt she thanked the steward and said good night to her companions as she stood to leave.

The others all gave her sympathetic looks as she made her way through the crowded dining room. Such a nice girl. Too bad she was stuck with such a loser.

Luckily the front office didn't close until ten and as she rounded the corner to the front desk she could see that she was the only passenger around.

"Room number, please," the lady said.

"2666," replied Brianna thinking again how appropriate the number was.

The receptionist quickly typed in the number on her computer and then printed out the page handing the copy to Brianna.

"Ms. James. There seems to be a lot of charges on your account today. We worried that someone might have stolen your key card. To be on the safe side we thought it best to contact you."

Scanning the large list of charges and reading the total of

$4,337.48 she was astounded. She recognized the drink charges from the last couple of days and today, but all the ones for clothes and jewelry she had not a clue. Surely Ron wouldn't do that or would he? And if so, what was he thinking?

"Ma'am, I didn't purchase any of these items. Is there anything I can do?"

"Well, we'll have to break-down exactly what was bought and where, but hopefully we can use the video surveillance to find out who has your card. It might take a couple of days. If any more charges appear we'll make a note of them and you can let us know if they're correct. Best thing to do is just drop by sometime tomorrow."

Thinking it best that the receptionist didn't know that she had a good inkling as to who the culprit was she thanked her and aimed her sights on the nearest elevator. She'd go change and then see if she could find Ron.

"So much for a special New Year's," she muttered.

Folding up the printout she mashed the down button and waited fuming. She couldn't suppress the urge to strangle that man. Of course she could be wrong, but not likely. How dare he take advantage of her again. Not that it was that big of a surprise, but considering she didn't have a job right now, surely he didn't expect her to pay for his foolishness. As the door to the elevator opened to an empty ride she stepped in and slapped the number two button on the control panel and continued her private tirade.

Knowing Ron like she did, she thought he wasn't thinking. Nobody was that dense or maybe she'd just met the king of morons.

The ride down was short, especially with her heated

mental conversation going. The door opened and she could see their cabin door from the elevator.

Quickly closing the distance between her and the door, she pulled out her key and paused thinking she'd heard a noise. Good, a confrontation in the cabin would be fine with her. Turning the knob and pushing the door open she was caught off guard by the scene before her.

There on the bed was the brunette girl and the king, himself. Looking about the room she noticed a variety of strewn clothing. Looked like she'd interrupted someone's private party.

"Oh, no! Bri, I didn't know you'd be back so soon."

"Who's the blonde, Ronnie, and why's she in your cabin?"

"I thought you could be a little more discreet, you idiot," Brianna yelled. Her temper having reached a boiling point. "I thought for some strange reason I could trust you, at least a little bit. You're no better than your father. In fact, you're just as crazy! Thinking I'll support your stupid laziness, while I work hard trying to supply you with the lifestyle you think you deserve." Reaching toward the bed as she said the last comments, both occupants cowered. Shelly huddled in the middle of the mattress, blankets pulled up to her chin, she was taking all these new facts in that this ranting woman was throwing her way. Watching in mute wonder as Brianna pulled out her luggage and began to cram things in.

"What're you doing, honey?"

"Don't honey me, you dork. You're in bed in the cabin we share with some floozy and you expect me to be okay with that?" Jerking open the next suitcase she started empting the rest of the drawers in a jumbled heap.

"Where are you going?"

"I'm taking my things and going to find another cabin to sleep in," she screeched. "You and your tramp can just enjoy this cabin as much as you like." Going into the bathroom retrieving her makeup, toothbrush, and other hygiene items, she stuffed all of that into the nearest bag. She then grabbed the door handle slinging the innocent object against the wall and marched out taking her belongings with her.

Ron stared in fascination. He'd never seen her show so much spunk. It was hot in some strange way.

"Ron, what was that all about? I truly don't understand. I thought you had money!"

"Well, it's a long story," he mumbled still digesting all the things Brianna had said before she'd stormed out. He still had no idea that she'd received the bill for his spending. Maybe she's just jealous.

"A long story. So you're just some bum! You mean she took care of you?" he just nodded in the face of this new onslaught. "That's more than I would have done and another thing. Without money you ain't got anything! You're a sloppy guy and a waste of space. I only stuck around you because I thought you were somebody. That poor woman! Putting up with your crap for so long." Crawling out of the bed, throwing on her clothes, and picking up her gifts she turned with the parting shot. "Don't expect me to acknowledge your existence anymore!"

Ron sat looking at the closed door. How could things have went so totally wrong? Shelly was out of the picture now. There went his retirement. He'd just have to cozy back up with Bri. If he bought her a present maybe she'd come around sooner. Besides, if she hadn't seen the bill already he could just sneak one more on the tab. He really had no comprehension as to what he'd spent. Couldn't be that much.

As he pieced together his new game plan he figured his best chances were to let Brianna cool off. Let her sleep on the ship in some uncomfortable chair and then she'd think better of leaving their little cabin. Meanwhile he'd just get some shut-eye. Thinking of Shelly right before he nodded off, he now saw how much work she would have been. He'd be better sticking with Bri in the long run. She was easier to handle.

After her initial tornado of anger tapered off, Brianna now saw how silly it was of her to leave the room. The front desk had now closed and all that was left for the night were the bars and some lounge chairs on the deck. She'd also left her key in her haste and couldn't even go back to the cabin if she wanted. Which she still didn't. Besides, Ron and his guest might still be there. At least she had put a nice rift between them. He'd obviously been playing her along. Now that the girl had seen the true side of him maybe she'd think twice about his companionship.

She'd forgot to mention the room charges, but that could wait until tomorrow. Ron wasn't going anywhere and since that girl now knew his sponge side, he wouldn't be buying any more gifts.

Deciding to pick the lounge chair on deck and dragging her things behind her to the nearest elevator she looked forward to the fresh air. The deck was all but deserted. Thank goodness. People would think she'd gone nutty toting all of her luggage around like a snail. Her temper took a while to build up, but when it did it exploded and always seemed to backfire on her.

She could have handled the situation differently, but other than being without a soft bed she was doing fine. In fact it was quiet liberating. All that anger had been piling up for ages. The torrent of verbal lava released so much pent up frustration both at herself and Ron. Looking back she could see that this should have happened a long time ago. Now was as good a time as ever.

Checking her watch with its Indiglo button she saw that it was nearing midnight. Almost a new year. She slowly leaned back in her chair trying not to mess her dress up since she didn't get a chance to change. The stars were just peaking through a filmy haze that was drifting across the ocean and onto the deck and she was getting sleepy.

The light night air had just picked up causing her still curly hair to flutter. Closing her eyes and letting the soft air caress her skin she could just imagine a new beginning. With that hopeful thought she slipped into a fitful sleep.

A dream was forming in her mind and she was floating, almost like flying, it was like thousands of little tingles were running up and down her spine. The sky took on a rosy hue and up ahead she could see a warm yellow glow. It was such a divine feeling.

She could see water below her and some of that fuzzy haze. Like a fog it rolled across the ocean in swelling clouds. Soon it obliterated everything else and all that was left was warmth she assumed was the sun.

She started hearing faint noises. At one point it sounded like voices and then changed to the creaking of wood and someone flapping sheets. How peculiar. What would someone be doing flapping sheets around? Why wouldn't they fix the creaking wood floor? Some oil or wax would do the trick. She then noticed the slow rocking. It had increased its strength from what she remembered, but was soothing. "What a nice dream," she sighed rolling over in her makeshift cot. The rocking reminded her of the hammock her parents used to have. Oh, how she loved to lie in that hammock and daydream.

The haze and fog began to clear. She heard a noise close by and jerked awake. Knowing that she'd gone to sleep on the deck and had evidently slept the night through from the looks of the bright sun she then looked at her surroundings. There were wooden crates on a wooden ship with two tall masts of sails billowing in the wind. Where was she and what had happened?

Her luggage had made the journey with her. Odd and odder, she thought noticing a note pinned to her bag.

It read:

One wish granted. Please enjoy. There is no going back now.
C/O star #265—location B.T.

Part II

The past is best forgotten,
The future burns bright and new.
It's time to start all over,
To wake to the fate calling you.
Don't dwell on what once was,
Follow where you heart leads.
An adventure waits around the corner,
And true love waiting to be freed.

FOUR

Gazing about in astonishment and pinching her arm, yes, she was awake and this was real. Around her were stacked different labeled crates: Fragile and Handle With Care.

"What kind of ship is this?"

She couldn't think of any shipping line that used sailboats. Looking up she could see two tall masts covered with thick tarp-like sails and there, to the left, swinging in the rigging, were two men doing what looked like mantinence.

Situated where she was, surrounded by crates and bundles, she was well hidden from most eyes. She wasn't sitting on the lounge chair anymore, a large pile of rope consisted as her new perch, which was rather comfortable. If she leaned a little to the left and craned her neck in the right way she could just make out the deck and a group of sailors.

What an odd assortment of people. Baggy pants and some shirtless, some with worn, frayed shirts, tall leather boots, and one guy had a patch on his right eye. It reminded her of a scene from a pirate movie. All that was missing was a bright colored parrot and the captain of course.

Speaking of the captain, a man who could be nothing but him had walked into her line of vision. He was tall with broad shoulders and burnished gold hair that curled and moved in the breeze. He had a lean tapered waist and was wearing tight fitting pants with a loose, flowing white shirt. The pants only accentuated his masculine physique, drawing attention to his toned form.

"I hope this isn't one of those cruises where they do reenactments," she murmured under her breath.

As she stretched forward to get a better view and hear some of their conversation, she failed to notice a small box containing farming implements. Bumping her shoulder into the box she stifled a squeal as it fell and ducked down as she heard the captain telling someone to find out what had made the noise.

Wally limped slowly over to the pile of crates. He'd been born with his left leg an inch shorter than his right and tended to take his time getting places. Especially since he wasn't a spring chicken anymore. He'd been in many scrapes over the years and always used the limp to take his opponents off guard. They figured he couldn't fight and was an easy target, but he soon proved them wrong. He was fast with a blade and had carved his fair share of injuries. His limp wasn't a weakness, but his age sure was catching up with him.

Wally had known the captain ever since he was discovered floating on a board in Nassau harbor. The boy, about five years old at the time, had been clinging to the debris of the *Fair Joan*. A squall had quickly come up, tearing the sails to shreds and taking the largest mast down. The boy was lucky to survive after a large wave then caused the ship to capsize and go under. He'd clung to that board for at least two days before ending up in Nassau.

His memory was gone and he looked like a drowned rat. All the boy knew was that his name was Daniel. It was stitched neatly into his torn shirt. He didn't know why he'd been on the *Fair Joan* or with whom. Luckily for Daniel, a local merchant named Richard Smithfield decided to take him in and help mold him into the fine man he now was.

Richard owned a small fleet, which carried supply goods to the various islands of the West Indies. He'd inherited his first ship from his father and continued to build a reputable shipping empire. He now owned seven of the fastest schooners in the Caribbean. He used the strict morals his father had instilled in him to run his business. Honesty and punctuality were his guidelines and he tried to raise Daniel to understand both their importance as a man and a merchantman.

Daniel had taken an instant liking to the trade. He was quick to learn and had good insight into people. Wally had been an employee of Mr. Smithfield for a few years already and when he met the up and coming Daniel they hit it right off. Wally worked at the harbor and longed to go back to the sea and as Daniel grew into a strapping young lad Richard gave him his first chance as a mate on the *Red Dawn*. He knew the boy would learn well under Captain Mitchell. So it was natural for Daniel to ask if Wally could join up too. He was only a mate, but Wally didn't mind. His mistress was the sea and he just longed to return to her bountiful waters.

Reaching the cause of the racket they'd heard, Wally put away his meandering thoughts and looked at the mess. Hand trowels, dirt scratchers, saw bits, and other metal objects lay scattered about the deck boards. Bending over to retrieve a spade close by, he saw a movement behind one of the crates. Peering over the mound of boxes his eyes grew round in confusion at what he saw.

A woman wearing what he guessed was a slinky black chemise crouched in a ball position and looked like she was trying to melt into the floor. Stowaway. Just great. And a woman at that. Everyone knows a woman on board ship is bad luck.

"What are you doing back there, lass?" he asked trying not to scare her further. When she failed to respond, he shoved at the crates until they created a small opening where he reached in, grabbed her shoulder, and hauled her to her feet. It was then that he took in her beauty. Long blonde hair, bright green eyes, and a thin lithe form. Even more bad luck.

Thinking it best to hide the frightened girl from the eyes of the crew he walked her to the captain's cabin. It wouldn't do to have the mates seeing such a beauty. It'd been too long since they'd seen a pretty face.

Brianna was close to having a major panic attack. Maybe this scruffy old man didn't mean her harm. The way her weird day was going, how was she supposed to know? As he led her towards a cabin, she wondered if she'd really lost her mind. Surely, this had to be a dream.

"Miss, if you'll just wait inside here I'll go fetch the captain."

She nodded her understanding still not willing to try her voice. What if they were pirates? What if they were kidnappers like in Brazil? She'd heard of people going there on vacation and disappearing. Then the family would receive a note requesting money. Her family didn't have any money.

In fact her closest living relative was a cousin from Utah that she hadn't seen in ten years.

The waiting was killing her. Trying not to panic. She sat gingerly on the bed.

"A stowaway, you said, Wally?"

"Yes, sir, and as you can see she's quite lovely."

Directing his gaze in her direction as they stepped through the cabin door, he had to agree with Wally. She was indeed lovely.

"Miss, I'd like to know why you're hiding on my ship."

Looking as confounded as she felt she said, "I really don't know. I woke up this morning and was here." She knew it sounded lame even if it was the truth.

Daniel had a chill run up and down his spine. That usually signaled trouble. Either directed at himself or for the interesting situation he now found himself in. He'd have to get some more answers from her first.

"Now, come on. We're not going to hurt you. Are you running from someone? Is that why you were hiding?"

"No, I honestly don't know how I came to be here. I remember falling asleep and then having a weird dream. I woke up surrounded by crates. You're not kidnappers are you?" she asked looking at them uneasily.

She felt it was best to keep her guard up. She'd answer truthfully as far as she could until they did something to suggest she do otherwise. Besides, she had nothing to hide.

Frowning with uncertainty, Daniel said, "No, we're not kidnappers. I'm a merchantman and we're hauling new supplies to my plantation in Barbados. My name's Daniel, Daniel Storme of the *Enchantress* and this here's my boatswain Wally Morgan. Can you at least tell us your name and where you're from? Maybe what ship you were on? We'll try to piece some of this puzzle together."

After hearing the ship's name, Brianna had goosebumps.

"My name's Brianna James from north Georgia," she managed to say shivering. "I was traveling on the ship *Enchantment,* headed toward St. Lucia. Maybe you saw it pass by. You couldn't miss it, a large black and white cruise liner from Florida with about twelve hundred passengers, not counting crew."

Daniel and Wally both thought she must've bumped her head and became addled.

"Ma'am, begging your pardon," Wally said, "but no ship can carry that many people. Are you sure it wasn't a fleet of, oh, say three or four ships?"

"No, Mr. Morgan, that's how big it was. I'm not exaggerating, it was in the brochure. ."

"Brochure?" asked Wally "What's a brochure?"

"You know. Like a mini magazine telling all the ships characteristics."

"Would you like one of my shirts to wear?" asked Daniel cutting off the questioning for now.

If she continued to stand there in that get-up he was sure he'd never be able to focus on the conversation. She had such long legs and such hair. A man could get lost in her hair alone. He shook his head to clear it of his runaway thoughts as she said, "Oh that's fine, but my luggage is on the deck. If you'd just let me get it I'll change."

"Wally, if you'd go get her things, I'll try to get to the bottom of this."

"Not a problem, sir," said Wally as he headed for the door. The poor lass sure was confused—a ship that'd hold twelve hundred passengers. What a crazy notion. And a brochure or magazine? Maybe after some rest her mind would clear.

Getting to the matter at hand.

"Would you tell me exactly what you remember? You said that you weren't running from anyone and that you fell asleep and woke up here," inquired Daniel.

"Yes, that's right. I had this fuzzy dream and jarred awake when I heard something nearby. I guess that's when I realized I wasn't where I'd fallen asleep."

Daniel started to feel that chilling sensation when he had a sudden thought.

It seemed illogical and even fanciful, but it was a hunch.

"What kind of dream did you have? We might pick up some clues as to what happened."

Tilting her head at him in thought she said, "Well, there was this haze that kept creeping in. There was lots of bright warm colors and I felt like I was flying."

As he considered her descriptions she continued to describe the now fading dream. He then moved toward his desk and the shelves beyond. He retrieved an old book he'd found in one of the many ports he'd visited as a young man. The book was titled *Mysteries of the Devil's Triangle*. He'd often been fascinated by the stories told from confused crewmen about the disappearances of shipmates and even ships they'd been traveling with. Christopher Columbus had even documented his crew seeing "strange dancing lights on the horizon" and about bizarre compass bearings in the area.

Considering they'd passed through the waters near

Puerto Rico last night, which were said to be the bottom corner of the triangle, he wondered if something of the paranormal might have occurred. He just had a feeling about it. Knowing the book almost by heart he turned to his desired page. This confirmed his strange inkling. He pointed to the page and she read:

> ...a fog that seemed to appear out of nowhere. The skies were clear, it being a night in mid-October. Our crew of twenty had no fear until the lights began. It was as though the sky were ablaze. Colors of red, yellow, orange, and even some I know not the name began to flash. Confusion and pandemonium set in. The compass upon the wheel started spinning about crazily and we prayed we were not due to die that night. Lashing ourselves to the masts in groups of 10 we hoped the spirits of those waters would let us pass.
>
> When morning dawned and we awoke not aware of when we'd slept, we noticed that four of our comrades were missing. How they disappeared is a mystery to us. The ship had floundered about without a captain. We were still securely bound to the masts. None of the crew could recall the other four untying themselves and leaving. It was as though the fog had swallowed them up. We reported our misadventure to the harbormaster in Nassau, but the story was written off as a "loss of crew due to bad weather." We'd not passed a gale or clouds in weeks. Only that fog.

The page went on about bearings and other reports. Her mind still felt too shocked to take all of this in. She'd completely forgotten the note she'd received upon waking. She'd mention that to Captain Storme. As she opened her mouth to speak, there was a knock on the door.

"Please don't mention our conversation to Wally. He's very superstitious and I don't want him worried overmuch. At his age it isn't good to have to many unexplained surprises."

She shook her head and decided to mention the note later.

Meanwhile Wally lumbered in carrying the oddest assortment of baggage that Daniel had ever seen. He'd seen his fair share in the shipping industry, but this took the cake. What kind of material were they made of?

Brianna smiled happily and thanked Wally.

He grinned back to see her so happy. She looked better already. Daniel must have discovered the problem and fixed it. The boy was so competent. If he were thirty years younger he might even give him a run for his money for the girl's favors. The luggage was odd and so was her speech, but she probably came from some far off place. Sighing he decided it wasn't for him to worry about anyways. Daniel could take care of it.

Rifling through her biggest suitcase Brianna thought how she would just love to have a bath.

"Captain, would it be possible for me to have a bath?"

"Sure, I'll have Tommy bring you some water and I'll come back later so we can finish our discussion."

Brianna thanked them both for their assistance and the two shut the cabin door on their way out.

"She sure is a pretty thing, ain't she Daniel?"

"Yes, Wally, she certainly is comely. We'll have to keep her in my cabin until we reach port. I don't want the boys to ogle her until she's had time to adjust. She still seems to be in shock."

"She must've hit her head or something. Poor thing's got her wits all knocked about. I'll make sure Tommy sees to her bath water and that he keeps his mouth shut."

"Thanks Wally. For now it's best we limit who knows about her. We'll figure out the rest once we reach Bridgetown."

Nodding and going in search of Tommy, Wally limped his way down the passage.

Daniel was left to ponder the things she'd told him. Thinking of the odd assortment of cases she had, he couldn't wait to speak to her further. What other interesting stories would she tell and where exactly had she come from? So many unasked questions. Not to mention how beautiful she was and that funny ensemble.

Brianna explored the captain's quarters. It was bigger than the cabin she had on the *Enchantment*. It was really freaky how she was now on the *Enchantress*. Creepy almost. Where would they hide the bathroom? Surely in the captain's private room he'd have one. And why would Tommy bring her some water?

Looking every place she thought it might be she still turned up with a negative. This guy must like to collect antiques. There were old maps, old bulky furniture, and a big walnut desk. There just wasn't anything here that she was familiar with. No magazines, soda cans, tennis shoes, or even jeans. Not that she was being nosy or anything. She was just looking for some clues. What if his crazy Bermuda Triangle idea was true?

What then?

He said he was a merchantman with a sugar plantation. She couldn't recall anything in her Caribbean research about any plantations in Barbados that still produced sugar. She could be wrong though. Maybe there'd be something on top or in the desk.

Feeling like an agent on *CSI* as she flipped through the scattered paperwork on top. Maps, charts, and schedules, but nothing about her at all. Then her gaze dropped to the latest shipping schedule. At least she assumed it was the most current. December 31, 1716.

"Seventeen sixteen, that couldn't possibly be right!" she exclaimed.

She heard someone nearing the door and then a discreet knock. Trying to quell her mounting worry she then moved to answer the door.

A young boy waited patiently to be allowed to enter.

"You must be Tommy," Brianna said.

"Yes, and I've brought your water, ma'am. It's nice to meet you." All this was said in a rush as he lugged two large steaming pails in. He turned back to the door and she heard a scraping noise that sounded metallic. In came Tommy carrying a large copper tub.

"I'll just sit this over here and you can add the water as you like. When you're finished just knock on the door. I'll be right outside if you need anything else. I'm your lookout. Captain's orders."

"Thanks Tommy. How old are you?"

"I'm nine ma'am. I just started as Captain Storme's cabin boy last month." Giving her a cheeky grin and heading for his post he turned before he exited and said, "I better go. I'm not supposed to bother you. You rest and I'll be a knock away."

That answered the bathroom question. Definitely old-fashioned, but it might be fun. Humor everyone at least for a while. Bending over the edge of the bed she could just make out a chamber pot slid out of view. Humoring people might have certain drawbacks. Until she verified the year she'd seen on the paper she'd do her best to relax. No use panicking unless you knew for sure. Who knows maybe it was a reenactment ship.

She gathered her soaps and fluffer from her toiletries, filled the tub steaming full and eased into the soothing water. Nothing like soaking away the tension; she'd just try to forget all this drama for the time being.

Her mind wandered to yesterday.

Ron was really doing his best to push her away. That suited her fine. She'd had enough of his using ways. Whenever she got this scrambled mess worked out she'd be sure to cut the chord.

Her mind then took another turn. What if she was in the year 1717? How then to cope with that?

Captain Storme's odd theory could prove true. Would she then be here forever? She recalled the small note that she'd discovered on waking. It'd said there was no turning back.

If so she'd have to deal with this change in her life.

Considering her lonesome state at the time this change took place maybe this was a hidden answer to her wish. Captain Storme certainly wasn't hard on the eyes and he was very understanding. Eyes that'd make any girl want to swoon danced before her. His were such a deep rich blue. The many laugh lines around them showed he enjoyed life.

Would she really miss much from 2007 if this was her new life?

Could she learn to fit into this new role?

A tingle rolled down her spine and she noticed the water had cooled considerably. Most would think it odd, but she had a strange feeling that she'd do just fine either way the situation worked out. She'd always been fascinated with history. Only now she might be part of it.

Deciding to leave the cool bath she started to rise and reach for her towel.

Daniel had discovered Tommy lounging outside his cabin door and decided the poor boy needed a break.

"Why don't you go get some food, Tommy and I'll keep watch."

"She never did knock, sir. She must've forgot . She sure is pretty." He said grinning his impish grin again and heading towards the galley.

Tommy was turning out to be a good cabin boy. He already had most the crew smiling at his silly antics. It was good to have a laugh now and again. Lightened the mood of the everyday.

It'd been some time since he'd spoken to Ms. James. He

now wondered if she was all right. He knocked gently on the door and when no answer was heard decided to check and make sure she was doing better.

The door didn't make a sound and he was glad in case she was resting. He wasn't prepared for the sight of her freshly washed skin glowing as she toweled off. He stood rooted to the entranceway wondering if her skin, which was the color of peaches, would taste like that wondrous fruit. Taking an uneasy step into the room he bumped into a chair causing a loud *scoot* noise to echo in the quiet room.

She jerked her gaze up and discovered him there watching her. She quickly grabbed the towel and tried to cover up her nakedness.

"Captain Storme! I didn't hear you come in."

"Sorry, Ms. James. I should've knocked first."

"It's okay. Really. I was just getting out of the tub. If you'd turn around I'd like to get out and dry off."

She sounded like a babbling fool. For some reason her mind couldn't control the speed of her tongue. Maybe it was because he was so male or because she hadn't been interested in a real man for so long, but for some reason she felt like the freshman girl in school that had a crush on one of the football players. He was so handsome and from his obvious appraisal of her body she knew he might be a little interested in her, himself.

When he gave her a lopsided smile and slowly turned around she rummaged through her things and pulled out a pair of jean shorts and a comfortable blue tank top. She then pulled out her flip-flops and was ready.

"Okay, I'm dressed now you can turn around."

As he turned around he caught sight of long shapely legs and couldn't stop his eyes from traveling leisurely upwards.

"So when do I get to tour the ship?" she asked.

When she asked the same question a second time he responded with a question of his own.

"What kind of ensemble is that? I've never seen a woman wear so little." Blushing and finally pulling his reeling senses together he looked away.

"I always wear shorts in the tropics."

"Shorts? Is that what those are called? It's a very appropriate name, but I'm sorry to say you'll be staying in this cabin until we reach port."

"Is something wrong with my clothes? I'd really like some fresh air."

"You're clothes, if that's what you'd like to call those, are not suitable at all. Don't you have anything else? Surely?"

Frowning with a feeling of impending doom she decided it was time to ask her big question.

"I was just wondering—ummmm—could you tell me what year it is?"

Knowing how stupid a question that was, she still waited holding her breath. From the way he reacted to her outfit she had a bad feeling that he was telling the truth about not knowing what shorts were.

Daniel knew the poor girl must have injured herself or was suffering from amnesia. She acted awfully strange. Of course he remembered when he was first found in Nassau. He'd be so confused and frightened. His amnesia hadn't cured itself yet.

Trying to ease the tension he now saw creasing her brow

he said. " Why don't you sit down and I'll answer your questions. I've some of my own. To your first, it's the Year of our Lord, seventeen hundred and seventeen. What else do you not remember?"

She was glad she'd taken the chair he'd offered. Amazing how hearing it up front like that took the wind out of you. How had she ended up on a different ship in a different time? More importantly, what was she going to do?

Her features had paled considerably at his answer. He could see her trying to come to grips with some fear or the other.

"Are you alright? Would you like some water?" He couldn't place what had made that fear appear. She seemed to be of sound mind and in good health. Other than her odd appearance and speech she looked normal. As normal as a girl of her beauty could look.

Handing her a small glass of water and watching her hand tremble his curiosity got the better of him.

"Would you like to tell me about it?"

That was nice of him to ask. To bad she had to freak him out, but somehow she had to start over. The note had said there was no turning back.

"It's very confusing, even to me." She started. "I'm not from this time-period. I'm from the year 2007. I don't know what's happened to me, why I'm here, or even what I'm going to do now." At his astonished look she thought to herself, great now he thinks I'm loony.

"I don't mean to be rude," he said, "but how do you expect me to believe all this? It seems rather farfetched."

Nodding, she understood. Farfetched indeed.

He appeared willing to listen. Might as well give him

the whole drawn out story. So she began at the beginning. Telling of her parents, her childhood, and Ron. Once she started talking everything tumbled right out. She talked for what must have been a couple of hours. Noticing how he paid attention, it made her feel like he was trustworthy. She didn't even know him that well, but he really listened. The last time she'd received that kind of audience had been with her parents.

"That's quite a story, but what of proof?" he said. Not as though he couldn't believe her, he could tell that she was telling the truth, as she knew it. What if someone did dispose of her because of a mental imbalance? The idea that someone would do that didn't sit well with his conscience. Even if she was touched, she should be taken care of. Family or friends or someone.

She'd been considering that question herself. How to prove such a fantastical story? Letting her sight wander around the room in thought her eyes landed on her luggage. Perfect.

"Let me show you my suitcases. I've things to show you that you've never seen or even dreamed of."

They both rose and walked over to where her things were located. He'd not paid enough attention to her baggage earlier. Such odd fabric and bright colors! He was fascinated. When she bent down and pulled on a small dangling cord and the teeth of the zipper magically opened it did seem otherworldly.

Brianna felt it was best to start it slow with her items. Now that she knew she was in the past, she could imagine how the smallest of her things could be viewed. Women of this time were burned for less. She pulled out her razor and the two romance novels she'd been reading.

While he fingered the burlap material that made up the case she smiled. He looked like a kid in a candy shop. Glancing her way when she began removing the chosen objects his brows rose in amusement at the bawdy covers on the novels.

Shaking her head, she figured it was just like a man to be drawn to sexual innuendos. He took the volumes in his hands and flipped the pages.

"I'd like to read these if you don't mind," he said.

She thought that might be a good idea. Give him some insight as to how writers did things in her time. Also the copyright in the cover wouldn't hurt either. One was 1996 and the other 2002.

Setting aside the books he then reached for her razor. It was pink and had four blades.

"Why would a woman need a razor?" he asked.

"Well, it's one of the customs of the twenty-first century for women to shave their legs and underarms. Sometimes they even shave other places."

Knowing a woman's anatomy well, he scowled.

"What other places?"

She gave him a meaningful look and he found himself coloring again. He'd never met a woman so open about sexualality. He could tell she wasn't a loose woman and from what she'd said about that Ron character he knew she was loyal. It would be nice to find a woman that loyal and giving.

Maybe her disappearing from that time was better. He couldn't believe he was entertaining the idea, but with the evidence before him he had to admit it was from some other place if not time.

He had so many questions to ask her and knew that she still had so many other treasures hidden in her bags. Looking at the clock he noticed how late it had gotten. He could just make out the lantern outside his door swinging in the breeze. It and the one in his cabin both gave off a warm haze making her hair burn golden.

It'd been a long day. He could barely resist the urge to touch her hair and feel it's silkiness.

"Ms. James, why don't I go get you a tray from the galley. I'll have Tommy bring it in and you can get some sleep. I had no idea it'd gotten so late. We have about two more days of sailing before we reach Bridgetown. Plenty of time for talking. We'll try to sort this mess out," Daniel said.

Brianna couldn't help noticing how the Captain sounded rather like he was nervous.

"Thanks, Captain, that does sound wonderful. I didn't realize how hungry I was until you mentioned it." Saying that her stomach let out a loud protest of its own.

Not wanting to leave, but knowing it was best for now, Daniel moved toward the door.

"I'll see you in the morning, then. I'll be bunking with Peter for now. He's my quartermaster. If you need anything else tonight just knock on the door and Tommy will be there on duty." With that he turned and left.

He seemed rushed or nervous she thought. How could she blame him though? She'd put him in an awkward position. He sure was handsome and smart. You could see the muscles in his thighs when he walked. When he'd helped her to sit in the chair, she'd put her hand on his arm and it'd been warm, hard, and toned. It wasn't easy to focus on her predicament when he was around. What would she do when they reached Barbados?

Returning her things to her luggage and walking over to the large bed she plopped down on the edge thinking that maybe after she ate and had a good night's rest everything would look better.

FIVE

After leaving Brianna so abruptly, Daniel strolled the deck deep in thought. It was amazing, but he couldn't help facing the facts of her story and the proof was so easily available. If she'd not been able to back up her claim, he wouldn't be in the condition he was in now.

She was such a beautiful woman. He admitted that. At first he'd thought her young, but he could tell that she wasn't a mewling schoolgirl. She had education, poise, and was comfortable with herself as a person. She didn't shy away from a man like young girls did. No giggling there. She'd looked him straight in the eye when he'd seen her toweling off. She did have modesty though.

As she'd told him about her past he'd truly been interested. He couldn't imagine a time when it was acceptable to live with a man and not be married. Especially when it was common knowledge that they were sleeping together. It saddened him to think of her losing her parents at what must have been a crucial time in her life. At least she'd known their love for a time. He still had no clue as to his own past.

The stars glowed up above and the moon cast it's glow across the deck. He could see some of the men enjoying the peace and solitude of the calm night. It was no wonder many loved the sea so. On a night like this you could feel that teasing pull of her lure.

For some reason tonight's beauty only made him want to help Brianna more. He had a strange urge to protect her. She reminded him of him years before. Lost and uncertain, but willing to try and succeed. He couldn't help believing that she was a fighter, her calm self-assurance and her struggling acceptance. He had to respect that. So how could he protect her?

The plantation in Barbados he'd purchased from an older man named Samuel Parker, who'd tired of trying year after year to produce the tiresome sugar cane crop. He was getting to old to fool with all the troubles. His son in South Carolina had asked him to move closer and he'd decided that now was a good time. It would be so much easier to see his five grandchildren that way. Besides with his wife gone these past two years the island just wasn't the same.

Daniel had given him a good price considering the plantation came with twenty acres and Mr. Parker said that he'd leave the majority of the furnishings, as he wouldn't need them in Charlestown with his son. That saved Daniel from having to purchase and transport the other items.

He had not yet seen the estate itself, but he trusted Mr. Parker. Richard had mentioned that he'd visited the man years ago when his wife was still alive and the plantation had been well maintained with a delightful view of the sea. With Richard's opinion in mind he had made the decision.

Daniel didn't know much about sugar and had heard that in Barbados the crop was on the way out, being outcropped by other islands like Jamaica. He had researched the sugar idea, but he could be persuaded on a different choice. His first matter was to find a competent overseer to help come up with the new ideas.

After asking around in the local taverns of Nassau, he'd discovered a currently jobless Duncan McCray. Duncan had been working on plantations since he was a lad. He had over thirty-five years of experience in cane, bananas, and other products. He was let go from his previous employer because his employer's wife had interest in him.

"I ain't dead yet, son. And the missus had a big hankering for some McCray hide. She weren't as purty as some, but she had an itch that needed scratchin. Mr. Donalds thought it best to let me go. He didn't blame nothin' on me. He just saw what the woman t'were after and told me that as he saw me as a likeable chap that it'd be best I find employment elsewhere before he had to do something about the missus."

"If you don't mind my asking, sir. How old are you?" Daniel had asked eyeballing Duncan's salt-and-pepper hair.

"Well, that's a fine question, lad. As you're in the prospect to hire me up I reckon you've a right to know. I'm only fifty-eight right now. I've a birthday coming up in July. Not too old to take on this here job you're offering. I've plenty of good years left as of now."

Daniel hired Duncan on the spot. He liked the man's candor. His honesty and obvious experience could prove very useful. Knowing how it was with his crew on the ship, Daniel felt that Duncan's loyalty would be an essential element in starting up the plantation to profit. He was a likable sort and would inspire trust from the workers. He preferred to pay his hands, not beat them insensible for forced labor.

Duncan had requested to be sent ahead to get a feel for how things looked at the new place. He wanted to have an accurate report as to what needed doing and what improvements should be made. He also wanted to get a feel for the soil and what crops might do well there. Sometimes planters tended to bleed the life out of the land and the crop that they'd always been growing wouldn't grow, the nutrients having been depleted. He reasoned from what Daniel had told him about Mr. Parker's problems that this might be the case.

Daniel had agreed whole-heartedly and had sent Duncan along with his housekeeper, Ms. Margaret Bryson. She was going to air the house and hire new servants to clean it and have it ready for the new owner. Margaret also found Mr. McCray, as she liked to call him, very agreeable. He was a decent sort and she'd not met that kind in a long time.

Thinking of the prospective match between the two brought Daniel back to the matter at hand. That matter was Brianna. He really liked her name. It suited her. Ms. James sounded so formal in his mind and knowing how lenient the future sounded he didn't think she'd mind.

He worried, because the people of Bridgetown were a close-knit group and like most small towns, reputations could be ruined in an instance. How could he possibly get her safely off the ship without the noisy gossip? That protective instinct churned again in his belly.

He reasoned that his crew was trustworthy, but even the most loyal crewman could spill information when he is in his cups. Maybe if he introduced her to them and explained that she'd been sailing in his cabin. They'd been at sea for almost a week now. That was sure to raise some eyebrows. If he only had a plan. A good safeguard.

If she were married and he were delivering her to a husband? That might work. It would seem odd though when no one met her at the docks, especially when she had no respectable clothing to wear. He'd have to find Margaret's trunks and fish around to see if he could find something for Brianna. Margaret was a bit more round that Brianna, but it'd just have to do for now.

Considering the different men on the island and the ones on the ship he suddenly had a sharp twinge at the thought of someone touching her. He couldn't just marry her off to someone he didn't know. He had to know that whomever he chose would take care of her properly.

He had a niggling feeling in his gut. Just why did he care so much what happened to her anyways? What kind of pull did she have on him? She was an enigma. He always liked puzzles. Maybe that's what it was, but somewhere deep down he knew it wasn't only that. It was bigger.

Sighing, he knew he'd have to tell Peter. His second in command was a logical man. He'd wonder at Daniel not sleeping in his own cabin. Peter was the only officer beside himself with a decent sized chamber. There was a pallet underneath his bunk that was used whenever Richard stayed on board with them. Richard wasn't much of a sailor and was getting up in years so he didn't travel too much.

The explanation would take some time to tell, but he was sure Peter would have a nice bottle of something they could discuss it over. Lord knew he needed a drink. Steady his nerves.

Knocking on Peter's cabin he waited patiently for the usual *come in* and when he heard the command he opened the door.

"Daniel, what can I do for you this time of night?" Peter asked.

"Well, I've had something unusual arise and will need to bunk with you for a couple of days. At least until we reach port. I'll explain everything in a bit, but first I find myself in need of a strong drink. You don't happen to have anything do you?"

"Sure, come in and grab a chair. I've got some good Scotch that I picked up when we were last in port."

"A little scotch would definitely help."

Sitting himself down in one of the chairs and waiting on Peter to pour the requested drinks, he had time to consider the story he was about to tell.

"So what kind of problem arose that you can't stay in your own cabin? Nothing wrong with the cabin I hope? No vermin or other infestation"

Knowing Daniel's penchant for cleanliness this was a common joke.

"No, my quarters are fine, but rather occupied right now. It's an interesting story although long. Your twisted humor should enjoy it immensely."

"By all means go right ahead."

Taking a sip of the fiery liquid for strength and letting the slow warmth seep in he nodded. The liquor seemed to be helping his tongue-tied condition.

Peter looked on in anticipation. It was rare indeed to see Daniel without the ability to speak. Watching his companion swallow the rest of the contents of the snifter in one quick motion he determined that the story must be good.

"Wally discovered a stowaway this morning. We heard a noise and I sent him to check it out. Turns out it was a woman and she's quite beautiful. Wally took her to my cabin so not to upset the crew. You know how suppositious they are and women are supposed to be the worst bad luck." Nodding and refilling Daniel's glass Peter waited.

"We tried to get some answers out of her and the ones we received were quite odd." Daniel told the rest of the story, leaving out the personal things that she'd told him. Things about Ron and her parents. It was his opinion that she wouldn't want everything known. "So that leaves me trying to figure out how to protect her. I know of no way to help her go back to where she was and she doesn't seem to be too worried about going back anyways."

What a crazy quandary indeed.

"I had an idea that if we could somehow acquire a husband for her that the gossips wouldn't be able to malign her."

"That's true, Daniel, but who would marry the girl and not think she was missing something upstairs? From what you've said, you believe her, but what would someone else think?"

He'd thought of that and it still plagued him. She wasn't crazy and he knew it. The proof she had wouldn't hold up to an angry tricked husband or even a town. Mobs had killed to many innocents for the entertainment alone and he wouldn't let that befall her. She was altogether different from the women he knew. Her accent could be played off, but her mannerisms and slang speech would be hard to explain.

"I do know of a great solution," said Peter. "In fact, it would take care of all our worries and protect the girl at once."

Peter had never seen his friend so enamored with a girl before. The story was weird and he was having a hard time believing it himself but he could tell Daniel did. He exuded the perfect picture of a smitten beau. A man shot down by cupid's arrow. It had finally happened to the untouchable ladies man and the poor creature had no clue that his wandering days were over. If he could play the cards right he could easily save the man from the torture of seeing the one chance at finding a woman who matched his character lost to another.

Looking at him with inquiring eyes "What pray tell would that be? I've worked my brain into kinks trying to figure out this tangle?"

"It's quite simple actually." He said fidgeting with his cuffs. "Marry her yourself."

He smiled when he saw Daniel's astonished expression.

"You said that you admire her. You think she's beautiful and you want to protect her. So marry her yourself. Richard's been after you for some time now to do that same thing anyway. It's the answer to all your worries."

Marry her. Was he ready for that step? Richard had been after him for a while now to settle down. It would protect her. His crew would think he'd been keeping the romance a secret as a surprise and he could use them as witnesses to the marriage. The people of Bridgetown wouldn't know the difference since he'd never laid foot in Barbados.

Maybe Peter was right. The idea didn't have as many negative aspects as it normally would. She was smart, comely, and different. Somehow that difference made up for a lot. He'd been called eccentric many times. It would only make sense for him to marry someone who understood. He somehow knew she would.

He'd never met a girl or woman for that matter that he'd even consider being tied down to. The many pleasing faces at the taverns and ports had become tiresome. They'd always wanted a commitment if he saw the same one more than once and he didn't want to lead them on or pick from the garish lot.

Now, thinking of Brianna as she was getting out of her bath, he could feel the stirrings deep inside. To touch that creamy skin. To hold that hot wet body close. Even to wake to her pleasing face. All those choices held positive feelings.

Pouring another drink and deciding to mention it tomorrow to her, he then looked back to his companion.

"Well, I'm off to bed. You can drink yourself into oblivion if you like, but you'll regret it tomorrow. Just think over what I said. It is a good solution. If you like you could look at it as a business relationship." With that parting shot and a crooked grin to himself Peter ambled towards his bunk. Before getting comfortable he pulled out the tucked away cot and pushed it to the adjoining wall.

The cot did hold certain appeal to Daniel. He was tired. The liquor had made him drowsy. He'd lie down and rest his eyes. Feeling the warm liquid fire in his veins gave him some relief from his confused thoughts. Noting the bottle's emptiness on the table he couldn't help thinking about Brianna's bright green eyes. He'd have to replace Peter's scotch tomorrow. It hadn't been his intention to finish it, but it relieved the urge to think so much.

The memories of peach-colored skin eased him into a fitful slumber. The decisions could wait. Happy dreams were all he'd seek for now.

A knock on the cabin door woke Brianna the next morning. Looking at the bright light filtering through the window she noticed how late it was. Must be sometime before lunch. Such a restful night. She didn't think she'd moved a muscle since she'd fell asleep.

As the knock sounded again she crawled lethargically out from under the covers. Pulling on a shirt that was hanging on one of the chair backs and approaching the door she discovered how it swam on her. The captain must've hung it there last night. She didn't remember, but oh well.

Opening the door she was pleasantly surprised by an always-grinning Tommy.

"Morning ma'am. Hope you slept well. I brought you some breakfast." He said taking in her attire.

"It smells wonderful. Thanks so much. What time is it anyway?"

"It's almost eleven. I thought it best to let you sleep. I snuck in earlier and laid out the shirt for you. Captain said you didn't have any good clothes."

"Where is the captain?"

"He's around portside checking on one of the sails. A

bird flew into it last night and got tangled in the rigging," he said placing the tray on the desk. "He said to tell you that he'd be by around luncheon to talk. He also said that he'd found you a dress in Ms. Margaret's things."

"Who's Ms. Margaret? One of the captain's lady friends or something?"

Giving her a quizzical look "No, ma'am. She's the captain's housekeeper for the new plantation."

"Oh," she responded. Eying the eggs and ham and feeling her stomach rumble, she sat down.

"I'll leave you to eat. Do you need anything else?"

"I think I'll be just fine. Did the captain mention anything to you about me, Tommy?" she couldn't help asking.

"He just said you were a friend that had crept on the ship without him knowing," he continued, "he also said not to tell anyone else on board. You must like him a lot if you followed him all the way from the Bahamas. If you don't mind my asking, how did you eat for three days? I mean you must've stashed food somewhere. And how did you sneak around without us seeing you?"

During this long tirade of questions neither had noticed Daniel entering the room.

"Let Ms. James eat, Tommy." Both jumped.

"You sure move around like a cat, captain," Brianna commented.

Daniel looked at the now subdued Tommy.

"Tommy, would you go find Peter for me and bring him here in about an hour?"

"Yes, sir."

"Don't worry, son. I'm not angry with you. We just have

a lot of things to discuss right now. You can ask Ms. James all the questions you like later. As long as it's alright with you of course." Sending Brianna a wink.

"That sounds like a good idea. We'll talk later. Okay, Tommy?"

He smiled his silly grin and nodded.

"I'll have Mr. Peter here within the hour, sir."

"He's such a smart lad," Daniel remarked after the door had closed.

"So captain, have you had any ideas as to my situation?"

It was so nice to meet a woman who got right to the point. No needless chatter about weather and such.

"Why yes, Ms. James. I thought long on the matter last night and with the help of Peter came to a simple solution."

Taking a bite of her breakfast she motioned him to continue.

"I'm sorry to bother you while you're eating."

"Oh, don't worry about it. I'll be done soon and this is important. Besides I'm on pins and needles."

"Well then. I considered all the options I could think of. Discarding each in turn as the negative aspects evolved." He sat across from her and steepled his fingers his gaze wandering to her mouth.

She chewed each bite with precision and licked her lips to remove the salt left from the ham. Unconscious of the effect her tongue was having on his senses she munched on. She glanced up at his pause.

"Is something wrong?"

"No, nothing. Just lost my train of thought."

"You were saying something about discarding ideas?"

"Oh, right."

She'd finished her meal and gave him a level look.

"Like I said before, I discarded most of the ideas when I considered their negative aspects. That was when Peter pointed out the simple solution." Scratching his hand and pulling his eyes off her he continued. "My conclusion to your situation was that you could marry someone. I considered the men on board and then the men in the port at Bridgetown and didn't feel they were quite what you'd look for."

Married? She just got to this era and that word already popped up. How could she marry someone? She only knew Tommy, Wally, and the captain. This was only day number two of her new life.

Daniel, not knowing her thoughts, but guessing continued, "I couldn't think of anyone suitable. That's when Peter recommended—"

"Just who is Peter anyways?" she interrupted.

"Peter's my quartermaster. My second in command."

"Oh, right. You told me that last night. So whom did he think of?" She was really trying to stay calm. No use getting mad at the marital pressure. She felt he would only have her best interests in mind.

"As I was saying Peter recommended that I marry you." At her blank look he then said, "I know it's sudden, but I find you to be an intelligent beautiful woman. It could work out nicely for us both."

Could she marry this handsome Captain? He hadn't thought her wacko even when she'd told him her amazing tale. He'd listened, considered options, and she knew he wanted to help. Like he said it might just work. Those bright clear blue eyes and muscles that went on forever. Shoot. She could do much worse and he was willing.

"I'm not asking for you to answer right now. I'll give you time to think over everything we've talked about."

Changing the subject to what he hoped was a lighter note.

"So what else do you have in your bags?"

Thinking how cute he was when he tried to be slick, she stood and walked to the bags in question.

"Well, why don't you come over here and I'll let you prowl around. Don't get too noisy though or I'll have to punish you." With a naughty wink in his direction she opened them up and he followed her over to where they lay.

She backed up and sat back down watching him finger her clothes. More shorts, tank tops, skirts, a few sundresses, then he reached her bikinis. He pulled the tiny garment out and quirked his eyebrow.

"What's this?"

"That's what you wear when you go swimming, although men wear shorts."

Didn't leave much for the imagination, but it would probably be fun. Next he discovered her underwear. Holding up a particularly skimpy thong on his hand he again quirked a brow.

"That's what women wear under their clothes. Not the most comfortable, but when you wear a sundress you can't see the lines." He didn't know quite what she meant about lines so he decided he'd learnt enough about her twenty-first century undergarments.

She got up, removing said item from his grasp, and said, "Okay perv, you've had enough fun fondling my clothes. Why don't you look at the other bag?"

"What's a perv?"

"It's short for pervert."

"I'm not saying you're one, it's just a slang word," she said, seeing his injured look.

"Slang word, huh? It's going to take me a while to understand your different words."

As he moved to the smaller bag containing her bathroom things she felt that was safer ground. Somehow, seeing him holding her underthings made her think of him taking them off. Slowly, enjoying every minute. Warm tingles started spreading throughout her belly. Her toes started curling in her shoes and wiggling.

"What's this do?" he asked, holding up a pair of nail clippers she then explained their use.

"That's rather clever. Much easier than a knife."

She had to agree. She couldn't imagine trying to alter her nails with a knife. She'd lose a finger or something.

About this time another of the many knocks she'd started getting used to happened.

"Sir, it's me and I've brought Mr. Peter."

"Come in, Tommy," Daniel said closing the case and standing.

Brianna had to smile at his *caught in the cookie jar* expression. It quickly disappeared as Tommy and the illusive Peter came in.

"Peter, I'd like you to meet Ms. Brianna James. Ms. James, this is Peter. Peter Swallows."

At that name she had to stifle a giggle. Surely, that couldn't be his name! It was like a porn star name in a dirty movie.

"Mr. Swallows, it's nice to meet you."

"Ma'am. Please just call me Peter. Everyone else does."

"Then I certainly will too." Turning around trying to contain her amusement she observed Tommy.

"Tommy, would you like to share dinner with me? I'd be glad for the company."

"That'd be great, ma'am."

Daniel sensed Brianna's amusement but could not place where it's source could be.

"I was just telling Ms. James about your great idea," remarked Daniel.

"It really was your idea, Daniel, you just didn't realize it until I pointed it out."

"Ms. James is going to mull it over and let me know her answer later."

"Ms. James, our Wally was asking about your welfare. What should I tell him?" questioned Peter.

"Oh, I'm doing much better. Tell him I'd love for him to drop by. The captain informed me I wouldn't be able to leave the cabin until port. So visitors are definitely welcome."

"Daniel, you didn't mention to her about the other part of the plan?"

Quelling this speech with a glance he looked at Tommy.

"Son, why don't you find Wally? I'm sure he'd like to know what Ms. James said."

"Sure, sir. Would you like me to bring him here?"

"After a while. We still have some things to get settled first."

Bobbing his head he went in search of Wally.

It was funny to see the captain acting so sheepish. He was usually such a charmer. Maybe Ms. James would tame his wild ways. Seeing the slim legs peeking from beneath the shirt she wore he could tell by her actions that she was comfortable in her skin. Her unabashed attitude was exactly the way Daniel had described and watching his friend he could tell that if she agreed to the marriage, it would be a learning experience for everyone.

"If you agree to my proposal I'll be able to introduce you to the crew and explain that I'd been hiding you. Keeping you to myself, so to speak."

The understanding spark in her eye proved the intelligence of which Daniel had spoken.

"Then I'll be sure to give you an answer soon."

Daniel turned around to look out the window. As he leaned slightly forward she couldn't help seeing his tight britches cling to his muscular butt. There was that tingling again. With an attraction like that, things were bound to be exciting.

Looking at the water, it was hard for him to contain his lust. It wasn't only the lust though. He admired her calm and she'd winked at him again. Her clothes had really shaken him up. Pictures of her wearing such items for him washed over his mind. She was such a mix of seduction, laughter, and intelligence.

Peter watched the exchange "I've got some things to check on if you'll excuse me. It was nice meeting you, Ms. James. I hope things work out."

"Nice to meet you too, Peter. I'm sure everything will be fine."

Daniel had the urge to run. Either run or explode from all the feelings he was having.

"Ms. James, I also have some things I need to do. If you'll

just think about everything and let me know. I'll leave you to your thoughts."

"I'm sure I'll come to a decision soon. My options are few so it should speed the process up. Don't look so worried. I'm not going to bite you." Unless you'd like, she silently added.

For some reason she felt like winking at him. Probably because it tore up his defenses. She could tell he didn't expect her to be in such good humor, but why shouldn't she be. A hot guy, no bills, and a chance to build a new future was plenty to put her in a flirty mood.

"Wally should be by later to visit," he said, stating what she already knew. He couldn't find his brain. It had evaporated at her subtle flirting.

"I'll look forward to it and dinner with Tommy too. I'll try not to let anything freaky out to the boy."

"I appreciate your discretion and I'll check on you later."

"Until later then."

She watched him disappear through the door in haste. She wondered if she should be so forward. Men in this time period weren't used to that. Her future looked so much better today. She'd tone it down a notch and see if that helped. She'd certainly flustered him.

SIX

The solitude of the day began to wear on her. She'd decided on her decision early. Dwelling on unimportant matters like what to wear for the ceremony made her realize how much of a girl she truly was. With so much time on her hands she might just go crazy.

Wally had dropped by for a quick visit and dropped off one of Ms. Bryson's dresses. He was all smiles at her assumed recovery. He could tell that the lass was definitely on the mend. The bright sparkle in her eyes made him hope the captain would discover what a jewel she was. Knowing the captain, it wouldn't take him long. Wally hadn't missed the stolen glances Daniel had been passing her way when he thought no one was looking.

"I hope this gown will do until we reach Bridgetown."

"Thanks, Wally. I'm sure I'll be able to make it work."

"I can't stay long," he said handing her the green frock. "You sure are looking much better, lass. I think the sea agrees with you."

She silently agreed. Things were working out nicely. The

dress although rather wide could be cinched in with one of her belts and the green shade would bring out the color in her eyes.

"I've enjoyed being at sea," she said nodding towards the window. "It's so vast."

"That it is. Feels as though you're the only soul about. Makes you glad to see your shipmates at times and at others you enjoy the solitude and beauty."

"Wally. Will you be staying at the new house in Bridgetown?"

"I'll be helping move everything from the ship to the house. So yes, I'll be up at the house for a spell. I'm interested to see what the McCray fellow has to say as to the plantation itself."

"Who's the McCray fellow?"

"That'd be the new overseer. He's a sensible man when it comes to production of a good crop. Has all kinds of knowledge about the land."

"Isn't the captain going to grow sugar cane?" she asked recalling that Daniel had said it was a sugar plantation. She also noticed that she'd taken to mentally calling the captain by his Christian name at some point.

"Well he was, but the old man who used to own the property said he couldn't get a good crop to grow. McCray's thinking the land's gone fallow."

She remembered in school when she'd taken agriculture that the ground did often loose nutrients, unless a rotation was developed to keep the soil renewed.

"Are there other crops that might do well or even better?"

"I'm a seaman, myself. Don't know nothing about growing things," he said shuffling his feet. "I figure if I retire, it might be good to have a garden. Course, I'd need a wife to tend that. I'd supply the fish and occasional meat." Odd that he'd tell her these secret thoughts. She listened so intently. Not jabbering away like a magpie as most women. He must be getting old.

Brianna thought his plan was a good way to go into retirement. She had always had a soft spot for older people. They often looked so lonely. The young people of the world buzzed by with no care as to passing up the slower. It discouraged her to think of all the parents and grandparents locked away in nursing homes. Out of sight out of mind.

"Guess, I'll head on. I'm supposed to keep a watch on Tommy. He's so energetic and tends to get to big for his britches," Wally said thinking he'd already said too much.

After Wally had left, she started thinking about this plantation. What would it look like? Would it be large or on a smaller scale?

She daydreamed a white two-story structure overlooking the sea. She could smell the beautiful flowers growing in the tropical garden. If she closed her eyes she could feel the cool breezes that would blow in from the ocean with summer thunderstorms full of lightning and heavy rain that would wash the humidity away leaving the air fresh and clean.

It did sound quite divine.

For now, she could try on her newly acquired dress.

Removing the large comfortable shirt and tossing it aside, she then pulled the green cotton frock over her head and tried to conform the many folds of fabric into some sort of order.

Opening one of her bags she pulled out a thick brown

Levi's belt. She'd preferred men's belts to women's since she was a child. For some reason the quality of material was better. Men did wear them more than women so she guessed that had to do with the quality of leather. Plain leather in a few choice colors was all they needed.

Luckily for her the captain had a nice mirror over his shaving stand. She could just make out the outfit in the small glass and it didn't look too bad after all.

Playing dress up had helped pass the time for a while. Soon Tommy would be by. She hoped it wasn't a long wait. There was only so much you could do within the confines of a cabin.

She wondered what she could talk to Tommy about. What did one talk about to a boy in this era? Fishing, maybe? Not cars, and he certainly was too young for girls.

Sighing her mind wandered again to the handsome ship's captain. How could she set up the scene to tell him her answer?

Recalling the various movies she'd seen and the romantic novels she'd enjoyed, it became increasingly apparent. She'd seduce his mind slowly and then see what would happen.

She'd go all out—hair, makeup, the whole deal.

Gathering together her supplies, lotion for soft skin, perfume for a light, flirty scent, and sultry makeup focused on her eyes. She started putting together the ultimate ensemble.

Tommy knocked on the door carrying a heavily laden tray. The cook had piled a lavish meal on thinking it was designed for the captain. His efforts would be enjoyed. Especially since the intended eater was the captain's future wife, who loved food.

"Tommy, I'm so glad you're here." Brianna said as the boy

stepped over the threshold, "I need an opinion." Doing a quick turn in the newly fitted gown. "How does this look?"

Depositing the tray on the desk and gazing in obvious adoration he said, "You look very nice, ma'am."

She had fitted the gown as best she could. Her hair was finished and fell in perfectly arranged waves down her back. Her makeup was done in soft greens with a hint of blush and a touch of pink lipstick to finish. She smelled of wild roses, which filled the room with the teasing scent.

Taking in her new attire Tommy was stunned. She truly was a lady. A fairy princess from the old stories Wally had told him of.

"So what's for dinner?" she asked taking a chair near the desk.

"Roasted chicken and potatoes."

"Sounds wonderful. If it tastes half as good as it smells I'll be in heaven. What do we have to drink?"

"I brought some wine, ma'am."

"Oh, Tommy. Please don't call me ma'am. It makes me feel old. Just call me Brianna, or Ms. Brianna if you like."

"Yes, ma'am. I mean Ms. Brianna."

By this time he'd recovered enough from his initial surprise to give her his customary grin.

"That's much better. So, do you know any jokes?"

"Jokes?"

She'd decided that humor was always a safe conversational choice when dealing with kids. Everyone liked to laugh.

"Yes, jokes. They're funny little riddles or stories that make you laugh." At the negative shake of his head she continued.

"I'll give you an example. What's black and white and read all over?"

He considered this seriously and finally gave the *I don't know* look.

"A newspaper," she said smiling, and he grinned.

Their dinner continued on with him telling her about some of the stories he'd heard onboard ship and her explaining the meaning of some and changing the subject on one's too advanced for his young age.

Needless to say there was laughter all around.

As Daniel approached his cabin door, he stopped to listen to their laughter.

She had a warm pleasant laugh. In a way, he hated to interrupt such a companionable evening, but on the other hand he felt drawn inside.

He opened the cabin door slowly so he wouldn't startle them and entered as they both turned in greeting.

The sight he beheld took his breath away. He was used to Tommy and had gotten used to Brianna in her odd clothes and the overly large shirt, but now she was transformed.

She stood as he came forward and smiled a slow, knowing smile.

"It's good to see you again, Captain." Her eyes held honest pleasure at his arrival.

"I hope your afternoon has been restful. I see you put use to Margaret's dress."

"It was a little big, but I've made it work."

She looked stunning to him and smelled of roses. He'd always loved the smell of roses.

"Tommy, if you'd leave us I'd like to speak with Ms. James alone."

"Yes, sir."

"Thanks for the company, Tom," Brianna said, as her sprightly companion exited the room.

"My pleasure, Ms. Brianna," he said, grinning again thinking of the new jokes to tell the others.

"Tom?" Daniel asked, giving her a quizzical look.

"Yes, he's decided that Tommy was too childish and now wanted to be called Tom. He said he wanted to be more like you and felt that a man's name would help."

"Well, he's still Tommy to me. One day I'll move on to the Tom, but for now he'll stay Tommy. Besides he's got too much energy to be just Tom."

She had to agree. Tom was to confining for his young exuberance.

Moving towards the desk where the remnants of the meal sat she picked up her goblet and started refilling her glass.

"Would you like some wine, captain?"

"Yes, that would be nice." Any excuse not to be staring at her lush curves hidden within the confines of her dress.

She handed him some wine and perched on the chair she had recently vacated. Daniel took her hint and sat opposite in the chair Tommy had used.

"I'll get right to the point," she said, fluttering her darkly lashed eyes. "I did a lot of thinking today. With my choices being so few and the differences of your time and mine being so many, I've decided to accept your offer. I had forgotten to mention a note I found when I awoke. It helped to push my decision. Even if it's just a hoax I feel comfortable with you and from observing you I think you'll be a wonderful teacher. I know I've got a lot to learn, but I'll do my best."

She took another sip of wine and slowly licked the warm liquid off her lips. This was going well so far, she thought.

Daniel had been watching her movements carefully and had barely heard her speech. She was so graceful that she didn't appear to know the effect she was having on him.

"I feel we'll do nicely together. You obviously are quite intelligent. Otherwise I'd probably be in a weird situation. Either raped or locked up somewhere." Sitting her glass down and gazing at him inquiringly, she asked, "So what do you think? Are you still up for the challenge? Meaning me, of course."

His mind couldn't stay focused. She smelled so good. So feminine and soft. The folds of Margaret's gown fell alluringly around her giving him the urge to loosen the belt and wiggle her free from the garment.

Her question caught him off guard. Trying to recall what she'd been saying he blinked until the full import of her statement sunk in.

She'd accepted.

The thought scared and excited him at the same time.

"Well, I think that's great." Wonderful. He sounded like a trained parrot or something. Then a puzzled expression crossed his features.

"You said something about a note? Could I see it?" he asked.

"Sure," she said pulling the small paper out of her dress pocket.

She smiled at his preoccupation. So far her seduction plan was working perfectly.

She reached over toward him, leaning ever so slightly forward to retrieve a breadcrumb that had fallen onto the desk during her meal with Tommy. Slowly she eased backwards with the innocent look of one who didn't know they'd just showed an ample amount of cleavage to her future spouse.

"I'm glad you're pleased. I guess we'll have to discuss the final plans for the wedding and I do so want to hear about Barbados." She toyed with her heart-shaped necklace that fell between her rose-scented breasts. "I still have a lot of questions to ask about you, you know?"

The oddest thought crossed his mind. This woman who he'd known for less than two days was flirting with him. Even hinted at seduction. If she continued along this course, he might just take up the invisible gauntlet she was throwing his way. Besides, she was now his fiancée and the note added more closure to their agreement.

He smiled and gave her a droll look.

"I was considering noon tomorrow for the ceremony if that meets with your approval."

She'd noticed the flash of interest that passed through his expressive eyes. She'd also noted the self-satisfied smile that creased his eyes at the corners. So he'd figured out her plan and decided on a counter-attack. That suited her just fine.

He also eased over to remove a crumb from the desk. His arms flexed underneath the soft cotton of his shirt as he slowly pinched the crumb and rolled it between his fingers.

"Noon sounds fine," she said, watching the play of various tendons and ligaments as they moved from his motions.

It was almost like he was picturing the breadcrumb as something else. Something on her body. The tingles started again. She could feel them dancing over her skin in teasing ripples.

The sultry look she was giving him made him want to span the distance between them and take her in his embrace. Smother her lips with hot kisses and caress each hidden curve of her body. She looked absolutely delectable.

She couldn't imagine what had come over herself. She'd never flirted this obviously before. It must be the wine. She'd always had trouble thinking while drinking wine. Funny, but it felt so good to let this secret inner self out some. She'd been holding back for so long. Either the wine or her nerves were making her giddy.

"I guess I'll wear this dress. Does it really look alright?" She then stood and walked a little around the room. "This is hopefully my first and last wedding and I want to look decent or at least presentable."

"You look lovely." In fact the only way she'd look better would be dressed the way she'd came into this world. "Don't worry about anything. We'll do the ceremony in front of the crew and then have another in Bridgetown if you like. You can get some dresses made and anything else you might need when we arrive."

"I'll certainly have to get used to wearing so many clothes. It's so hot here." She did a turn and winked his way.

Daniel had glanced over and noticed the now empty wine bottle. His intended was obviously very close to being foxed. She made quite a picture. Smiling alluringly and turning about.

He needed to leave before he forgot all his reservations.

The longer he watched her twirling about sending him hot looks and winking the less likely he was to get out of this room unscathed. He started feeling like he was being hunted.

When exactly did the tables turn on him? He'd thought he could handle any of the coyest lasses. Of course he wasn't to marry them and the attraction hadn't been near as strong.

As she made one last slow turn she looked him straight in the eye and knew that she had him right where she wanted him.

It was then that a decidedly loud *hiccup* escaped her lips. Causing her to grin again.

He looked so sweet trying to fight the rising fire she was igniting.

A thought popped into his mind. Patience. Brianna had been used and hurt so much in her past. He wanted to make this right for her. Like she said she was only planning to get married once. Best to make it totally right for her.

Before she could protest he stood. Offering her a simmering look full of promise. "I think I'll call it a night."

At her wounded expression he felt compelled to explain.

"You've been sorely used in the past and I want our marriage to start out better than that. I already respect you and because of that I must leave now."

As the understanding dawned in her mind that he could be so caring he saw the faint trace of tears appear within her green eyes.

"Thank you for thinking of me that way. It's still strange to me to realize that men can be chivalrous. I'm so used to the other way around." She wiped the moisture away from her eyes and continued. " I'm not used to people putting me first. Especially men."

"I know that and I also want you to know that you've tempted me almost to the brink, but I can wait until tomorrow. Although gallantry seems to have been lacking in your life. I'll make it a point to insert as much as possible in your future."

Lifting her small hand in his and placing a chaste kiss upon the back of her wrist he bowed and said, "Until tomorrow my fair maiden." Then he turned and left the cabin.

Brianna was left to ponder the kindness of this man she was to marry. She could still feel the warmth of his lips on her wrist. He was certainly a large combination, like a frosted cake. It looked wonderful on the outside and as you cut out a slice you could see that the inside would be just as good.

To think that he'd twisted her seduction attempt into something so much nicer. Gallantry. It was a complete change from what she was used to and she had to admit that it made her feel important. He really was worried about making this situation into something they could both cherish.

The wine and these thoughts gave her a warm cozy feeling. One she hadn't had in a long time.

Leaving Brianna in the cabin by herself had been one of the hardest things he'd ever done. The thought of disgracing her like a common trollop didn't sit well with him.

When he'd first laid eyes on her she'd appeared like a lost waif, not truly a woman or a child. That was completely banished by the impish lady he'd just encountered.

A feeling of correctness and something falling together from a larger plan washed over him. It mattered not to him what odd trick of fate this might be only that he could keep this treasure he'd found. Maybe he'd finally found a puzzle piece that could help fulfill the loneliness in his life.

Although he still didn't know his childhood past, it no longer mattered as much. He now had someone he could talk to about loss and knew she'd understand. Having lost her parents and wasted so much time with people who used her she'd be very understanding to his thoughts.

Heading towards Peter's cabin he looked forward to tomorrow. A good night's sleep and a good breakfast and he'd be ready for anything.

Brianna couldn't help but feel a little frustrated at Daniel at having left her alone. She understood his reasons and thought them to be thoughtful, but her other side, the lonesome side, still wished he could have stayed. It would have been so soothing to have had his arms around her. Not just the physical release that would have surely happened, but the physical comfort of someone holding you. Being there for you as both a mental spirit and a physical closeness.

To think that tomorrow at this time she'd be a married woman. Mrs. Daniel Storme. Brianna Storme. The name sounded so smooth. It just flowed together.

Glancing in the mirror she had to admit the gown did look elegant. The material wasn't anything fancy, but compared to her future clothes it seemed to fit in much better.

"Must be the fact that it's so different a style," she mused out loud.

Which brought to her mind that she tended to talk out

loud to herself a lot. Hopefully, Daniel wouldn't mind her silly ways.

Ron had often commented, "You never know who you're talking to. You mumble like a loon gone loco and what's really bad is you answer yourself. You'd think the conversations were interesting or something."

He'd not been a big fan. Especially when his shows had been on.

Now that she thought about it. She didn't miss the creature comforts she'd left in 2007. Must be adaptation kicking in. So many of her science classes had said that those that didn't adjust would whither away.

Now that she would have a husband and a home on one of the nicest islands in the Caribbean, her future started to change and in a way look more promising.

Who would have known that a silly wish on a sparkling star would become a reality?

I guess that just goes to show that it never hurts to dream, she thought.

Slowly, she undid her belt and removed her new bridal gown, laying the garment across the chair back so it wouldn't wrinkle. She smiled into the mirror over the stand and eased her way to the bed.

She wasn't there for ten minutes before her eyelids started closing. Snuggled beneath the soft quilt and the fluffy pillows it was no wonder her dreams were of a certain golden captain with eyes the color of the morning sky and hair that glowed with a warmth from within.

SEVEN

As dawn's soft caress floated across the morning sky, a shaft of light shot through the window where Brianna lay sleeping. It had been a long night full of worries and excitement. She'd felt like a child getting ready to leave on their first trip to Disney World. So filled with anticipation that she couldn't sleep until her body just wore out and the sandman said it was nighttime. She had no clue that she'd slept so hard. She had no memory of falling into the oblivion of sleep.

Blinking to clear her eyes, she sat up to escape the bright shaft of sun. Thank goodness the night was over. Part of her wait was now out of the way. She was so lucky she wasn't late for work. Those days were now her past and she could easily say she didn't miss that part.

Weird to think that her past was the actual future and that now the past was her future. This would have made a great episode of the *Twilight Zone*, she thought.

Rising from the bed she went to look out the window. It certainly was a beautiful morning. Just the kind you'd want to start out your wedding day. Must be a good omen.

She wasn't one to dawdle, so she started getting around to wash up and dress for her special day. She could only hope to concoct something beguiling with her appearance.

Daniel had slept well. His early doubts had been squelched by a dream he'd had.

In the dream a kindly couple had smiled benignly at him. The man had the same bright blue eyes as Daniel's own and the same burnished hair. The lady held herself with a stately grace and her own gray blue eyes lifted at the corners in happiness. They'd both hugged him and said they were proud with his choice.

"She's a fine woman," said the man.

"We couldn't be prouder."

He'd awoken with a comfortable feeling in his chest. Although he still could not remember everything from his childhood, he couldn't help feeling he knew the couple. If his instincts were correct it'd been his parents.

He'd drifted into sleep again after this first dream with some memories uniting from his past to float within his mind.

He remembered the day as one of those wonderful summer days out of all the childhood daydreams. Hardly any clouds covered the sky and the bright sun glistened off the harbor.

A lady moved slowly into the light of the garden to hold his hand. He now recognized her as the lady from his previous dream.

Their view of the harbor was perfect. The ships floated to and fro. Bobbing gently with the flow of the current.

A tall man waved to them from one of the largest ships. He smiled from ear to ear and as he neared the lady beside him gave an unladylike whoop of joy and ran out of the garden towards the waiting arms of the gentleman. He could remember not being to far behind her in the run to reach this long missed man.

The man lifted him into the air saying, "Look at you, my son. Growing like a weed! I'll bet you've been eating well."

"Yes, John. He's particularly fond of Cook's sweets."

"He can't help the sweet tooth. Runs in our family. I know I can't resist sweets either. I mean look at you, my lovely Sarah. You're enough delightful sugar to keep me sated for years." All this was said with a wink to young Daniel, who'd now been placed upon the ground.

He couldn't help grinning at his father's unabashed love of his mother. In fact he couldn't blame him. She was certainly sweet both in nature and love.

With an unexpected hoot his father grabbed Sarah up in the air spinning her and saying, "I've wonderful news to the both of you."

At the conclusion of this craziness he could hear himself say, "Oh, tell us please, Father!"

"Well, my inquiring Danny Boy I'll not be leaving again. I'm home for good."

"John? Really and truly? No more long absences?"

"Yes, my love. I'm retiring. I've had enough of adventure for a long time. I'd also like to see this boy grow into a bright young man."

"I'm so happy right now," she said. The tears in his mother's eyes glistened like diamonds.

"And that's not all, my lovies. I've planned to take us on a holiday cruise. I thought it'd be nice to visit some of these beautiful Caribbean isles at our leisure. Explore some with the two I love most."

Later that night sitting around the dinner table enjoying Cook's delectable food, they discussed their plans and where they'd be visiting.

The night wore on and wore out the young Daniel. The last thing he heard before he drifted to sleep sitting in his chair was, "I'm so glad you'll not be off adventuring anymore, John."

"It's good to be home. Hopefully before the year's out we can give Daniel a baby brother or sister. It's good for little 'uns to have company."

"Yes, it is. Maybe we can start trying tonight," she responded with a subtle blinking of her eyelashes.

Noticing the dozing Danny Boy, as his father liked to call him, the two smiled. John lifted the light burden of his four and one half year old son into his arms. It'd been hard these past years at sea. He'd seen and done many things he regretted, but never would he regret this love he had for Sarah and the gift she'd given him in their son. Daniel was a sturdy little fellow and would make any man proud.

As he lay the boy down for the night his heart sent a prayer to heaven to safeguard this child. This boy was the fruit of such a beautiful love. A love he'd almost lost. Sarah was everything to him. It just took him too many foolish years to realize the treasure he'd had at home. Jewels and gold were not enough to fill a man's soul. Especially when he ended up in a watery grave.

Daniel awoke that morning to the gentle rocking of the ship and he would have sworn he could still feel the strong arms of his father as he'd whispered the prayer above his semi-conscious form. He smiled to himself as the memory of the dream played over in his mind.

He now knew his parents' first names and that they'd loved each other dearly. They also told him they were proud of him. It depressed him some to know for sure that they were dead. He'd always harbored a slight hope that one day he'd discover them alive and that they'd been searching for him.

It was good to have the closure. He'd have to tell Brianna about the small insight into his childhood past. Maybe one day the rest of the pieces would meld together.

Deciding to leave his thoughts for more pressing matters. He set about informing the crew of the luncheon nuptials and from their amused faces it seemed the knowledge of a certain green-eyed enchantress had leaked out. Not that it mattered now. The crew was pleased for any reason to enjoy a celebration.

He'd saved many of them from working in terrible conditions or worse, being taken by slavers. All had a reason to wish Captain Storme well and they looked forward to the meeting of is new lady. A lady who from a report from a conversation overheard between Wally and Tommy was a veritable fairy princess.

The deck was strewn with anxious faces. Each awaited the appearance of the bride.

Watching the gathered group with a comical eye stood

Peter, the best man. Wally would do the honors of walking Brianna down the deck to meet her bridegroom.

Daniel looked splendid in his navy velvet coat with nautical gold tassels. Black knee britches and shiny tall boots completed his matrimonial ensemble.

As Brianna met Wally at the door, butterflies danced crazily in her stomach. She'd not eaten for fear of disgracing herself and had enjoyed some hot tea to sooth her nerves. Now as her belly did somersaults, she was glad she'd not partaken of the meal that Tommy had brought by.

Wally couldn't help admiring the beauty of Brianna. It'd been a long time since he'd seen such coloring and such gracious manners. The women at the docks would be green with envy if they could see him now. He was glad the captain had snatched this one away. There would have been competition plenty if the men around Bridgetown could have courted her. She'd have brought every plantation owner, shipmaster, banker and sailor to her doorstep wishing to win one of her intriguing smiles.

Brianna gazed at the assembled crew as they made their slow progress toward Daniel. From their awed expressions she must have done well with her toilet.

It'd taken the best part of the morning to complete, but it was worth it. Now seeing Daniel's warm perusal and the heat that flamed from his eyes she could only look forward to the night ahead.

Wally stepped forward and placed her hand within the gentle grasp of Daniel's. He looked down into her eyes and then turned his attention to the task at hand.

"Gentlemen, I'd like you to meet Ms. Brianna James, my

betrothed. We both want to thank you for bearing witness to our marriage."

"Yes, thank you all for understanding our secretiveness. Sometimes it's easier to leave your past and start anew. We both hope to make a lasting try at starting new together," Brianna said smiling at the assemblage.

It had been explained that Brianna's family weren't in agreement with the match and in a desperate attempt for them to be together she'd been hidden away on the *Enchantress*. Over all everyone thought the idea romantic and that it was with great fondness that they watched the joining of the two.

And so the ceremony began.

"Ms. Brianna James do you take me, Captain Daniel Storme, to have and to hold, in sickness, and in health, 'til death do us part."

She felt an encouraging squeeze on her hand and said, "I do."

Glancing into his eyes she could barely conceal the joyful glow she now felt at saying those words. It was like a bird within her had taken wing and she was free to live life to its newfound fullness.

Daniel sensed the happiness that radiated from her words. Such all-consuming trust that she'd given him pushed him to continue.

"Brianna, I Daniel Storme do take thee, to have and to hold, in sickness and in health, 'til death do us part."

Having said that he grinned ruefully to the on looking crowd.

"Being that we did rush things a bit, I'll have to skip the

ring part." Then to an aside directed at Brianna he said, "I'll try to purchase something in Bridgetown to match your eyes." Then to the crowd again, "Now I may kiss my bride."

He carefully leaned over and cradled her head in his hands kissing her lips with a soft caress.

"Aw, come on, Captain, you can do better than that," shouted Roger, one of the mates. "She's a might purty to waste on a nibble."

"Aye!" shouted the crew in agreement.

Whispering into her ear Daniel said, "I guess the men want more of a showing. What say you, wife?"

"Aye, Captain," she whispered back breathlessly.

So to the joy of the crew he then gathered her in a tight embrace delivering a thoroughly sound kiss. Then sweeping her up into his arms he shouted. "Don't bother us until you sight port. We'll be indisposed for the rest of our voyage."

The cheers of the crew followed the retreating figures as they made their way to the marriage cabin.

Daniel pushed open the cabin door, carefully carrying his wife across the threshold. He quickly noted that a tray had been placed on the desk with a large chunk of cheese and a fluffy loaf of bread. A bottle of wine and two crystal goblets finished the meal. It appeared that everything had been taken care of to his specifications.

Depositing Brianna upon the bed he still continued to wonder at this sudden state he found himself in.

He lit two tapered candles and drew the curtains closed to set the special ambience that he sought.

Brianna watched all this in delighted amusement. So much trouble he went to on her account. Her husband. The grace of a restrained animal showed in his deft movements. A tiger maybe, she mused. He reached the desk and began pouring out the wine into the goblets. Then crossed the room with one arm outstretched for her to take a glass.

"Shall we do a toast?"

"Yes. Let us. But what should we toast to?" she inquired giving him an innocent look.

Her coyness amused him and brought to mind a conversation he'd had with an old sea dog.

"The sea's a wild mistress," the man had said. "Full of changing moods and temperaments, but there's not a chance that I'd leave her. She's as addictive as opium."

At the time Daniel had just nodded in agreement, but now he knew the truth of the man's words. Somehow he knew he'd feel the same way about Brianna if she were taken from him. Her fresh honesty and sharp mind wetted his appetite to know more about her. Her beautiful body only complemented her soul. His soul wanted to reach out and claim her as his. Forever.

"Let's toast long life, good health, and to taking chances no matter how unexpected they may be."

"Also," she said eying him covertly, "to us and our future, May it be full of joy."

Clinking the glasses together in salute the glasses were quickly empty again. A warm silence fell. Both lost in thoughts of their future.

"Shall we begin this adventure?" he asked removing the now empty goblets.

She nodded her head and laughed.

Finally all her pent up emotions could be let loose. She knew that within the arms of this charismatic man that she would find a safe haven of protection from all that had been and would be. She'd found her haunted knight. It was up to her to free his trapped soul.

His hand trailed the curve of her cheek leaving a path of tingling fire. Her breath caught at the sweetness of the caressing gesture. His eyes blazed with an inner passion that cried out for her to fill. Her heart started to race madly within her chest and her eyes closed as he began placing strategic kisses along the nape of her neck.

She'd wondered if the romantic nonsense in her books were ever true. She'd even doubted the sanity of the writer's minds. Such bliss could only have been conjured in the thoughts of daydreamers. The truth of their stories opened within her.

Gentle touches and soft lips could indeed move the soul.

Daniel felt the nervous tension in Brianna slipping away. He'd known from the first that she kept her passion hidden. It had been his goal to free it from the labyrinth within her.

He'd never expected to crave the battle as much. Each butterfly kiss, each nibble and lick were aimed at a more intense and satisfying lesson in love.

Their surroundings disappeared until all that remained were their two bodies and souls wrapped in the ageless dance of loving. It was the joining of mind and body, a complete marriage.

After their second bout of lovemaking and a snack of

bread and cheese, they settled in to bask in the glow of each other's love.

Darkness had come long ago and the ship was embraced in the warm folds of night's velvet darkness. The mates had celebrated heartily for their captain. They sensed a deep passion brewing between them and could only envy the Captain's luck at finding such a tasty morsel.

Bridgetown port would see them docking early the next day and all aboard were pleased to see the end to their week-long journey.

The discussion in the cabin had moved from family memories to what they'd do once they docked.

Daniel told Brianna that once there she could visit the local dressmaker and order a complete trousseau that could be sent to the plantation as the dresses were finished.

His continued thoughtfulness still amazed her. Ron would have never cared like that. The closeness that they'd both felt at their first meeting had grown deeper on as their magical day had developed.

He'd told her of the dream he'd had about his parents and she expressed joy that he'd discovered something so dear that'd been previously lost. She hoped that this dream would be a starting point for the total recovery of his forgotten memories. Memories that now were revealing the wonderful love of his parents and of who they might have been.

He wasn't sure what had occurred, to cause the loss, or what had caused the sudden memory to appear unrepressed whether it was a knock on the head or something more traumatic. One day the explanations would appear.

Brianna explained some of the interesting shows she'd seen on the *Discovery Channel* about amnesia. She'd had to explain the television in detail, also. She regretted not knowing the cure, but did enlighten him that sometimes places or objects heightened the memories recovery.

Overall their conversations were full of interesting things. Hers were full of future knowledge, which Daniel found fascinating. His conversation contained a living history that Brianna couldn't get enough of.

She was consumed with a strong urge to make this complex man happy. He was in turn consumed with the same urge for her.

From Brianna's viewpoint, she knew if they both worked on it with trust and understanding they'd do very well. That was one of the big messages from the popular *Dr. Phil.* She usually found him silly. In this respect she felt it did make sense. Trust was ever important and above all honesty.

Daniel detested liars and so did Brianna. Together they made a pact to be honest with each other, no matter how terrible the truth. Things could be worked out.

Brianna had discussed how marriage and divorce ran amuck in the twenty-first century. That it wasn't strange for people to divorce and remarry and do the same again if it didn't work out.

To her it had been a mockery of the vows. Some things were indeed sacred. Hollywood tended to overlook important things like that as being inconvenient.

After talking with Bri, as she'd told him to call her, he was glad he had missed all of the future mess. From the stories she'd told him it looked like people had lost sight of what was important and who. He was just glad he'd never have to witness all the waste and excess. It reminded him of how many monarchs over indulged and left the poor to wallow in their grime. Not the best of metaphors, but it matched pretty well with how he pictured her time.

EIGHT

Enchantress arrived in harbor just shy of sunrise. Once the ropes were secure and the gangplank in place the ship was set to start its disembarkation.

Peter gave the orders to the crew on what to unload first and Daniel left a dozing Brianna, in search of Duncan McCray. Duncan had been assigned the task of meeting the ship with wagons and a carriage to take the various objects up to the plantation.

Daniel located Duncan in a small tavern just off of Broad Street.

"Ah, Captain, I'd just arrived and sat down to whet me whistle. Thought I might grab a bite to eat, but seein' as how you're already here, I'll leave off."

"That's good of you," commented Daniel.

"I hope your voyage went well, sir."

"Indeed, we ended up having quite an interesting trip," he said giving Duncan the story of his new bride.

"Well, you seem no worse for wear from your tangle with the matrimonial web."

"Yes, well, the spider wasn't as bad as everyone had portrayed it," Daniel said, giving him a wide grin.

"That's just after one day, sir. If you don't mind me sayin',' still plenty of time yet for the spider to devour you," Duncan said in exaggerated seriousness.

"Quite true, but even so, the journey will be worth it."

"I'm just glad your happy, Captain. Everyone deserves some happiness." With that said he drained his pint. "I'm sure your ready to be gone, so I'll not hold us up no longer."

"How's Margaret doing up at the house?" he asked as they walked down the boardwalk.

At this query he saw a blush creep up Duncan's blustery features.

"She were fine last I saw her. That's one woman that'll do well anywhere. She's all spittin' fire one day and nice as posies the next. Never know which way her winds blowin' until the breeze starts," he remarked, wiping the sweat from his brow. "By then, you've no time to run for cover. I swear I'll never understand women."

From this long-winded confession Daniel guessed him to be quite smitten and knowing Margaret, he knew she'd put Duncan through his paces.

"Now don't get me wrong," continued Duncan "She's a good figure of a women. It's just she's got a tempter like a cat with his tail shut in a door. All claws and hissin' and such. Don't take nothin' to set her off neither. Then again—" he said cocking his head in a thoughtful expression, "I can't blame her none when I like to poke the embers to see how long it takes to catch. It's excitin.' Well enough of that. I do go on. Let's go fetch your lady and the goods and be off. I've a sudden urge to add some lumber to the coals."

Fidgeting in his pocket he tried his best to keep the jewelers pouch hidden, but Daniel had seen the Barbados Diamond's emblem during Duncan's frustrated attempt to dab the sweat with his handkerchief.

He certainly was an old scalawag. Clever enough to know when to arrive home with a peace offering. He could just picture Margaret's face. She'd go from scarlet anger to joyful tears. The two would make a charming match. They'd just have to get through the preliminary troubles.

It was from a grogshop across from the tavern that Daniel and Duncan had just vacated that a crabby old man named Lefty spied the two. At first he couldn't believe his eyes, but on hearing Daniel speak his ears confirmed what his eyes already knew. He'd finally found John Hammock's whelp. That whelp being Daniel Storme.

That long ago sacking of the *Fair Joan* had been one of his failed attempts to eliminate a problem. Once a crewman joined the ranks of the *Plunderer* the only way out was death. John Hammock didn't understand this. He'd been a member of the crew for three years and had decided to retire form the sea life. He had missed his family.

John had wanted to right some of the wrongs done from the *Plunderer* and it's Captain, Lefty Shakes. Retiring had been his way of starting over. He'd saved casks of treasure from his share of spoils and wanted to move on. Start up fishing or planting. Anything but killing and pillaging. Those days were out of his system.

Lefty needed to dissolve the existence of Hammock. He would kill the wife, child, and Hammock in one fatal blow.

Unfortunately for Shakes on the day of the sacking, John, in a last chance of saving Daniel after seeing Sarah knocked down, threw the boy overboard before the other crewmembers of the *Plunderer* saw. Daniel bobbed quietly out of sight. When he heard shots and saw the flames, he remained silent. He knew evil was close by and he did not know about his parents.

It was with great pleasure that old Lefty Shakes now saw his future prey. No one escaped the wrath of the famous Plunderer's Captain. Especially after John Hammock had robbed him of the ability to enjoy women. He could still feel the scar where Hammock's blade had severed the vein to his lower abdomen. The blood loss alone had almost killed him.

This was his last chance to kill the one person who remained that was held dear by the man, Hammock. The man who'd made him suffer so for so many years.

He'd round up a crew and explain his ideas. Get them all stirred up for blood and throw in a hint of treasure. That never failed to intrigue the nastiest of pirates.

Either way this man who was the lost son of Hammock would pay and dearly.

Daniel remained clueless to the plots of revenge brewing in the grogshop. He arrived at the ship to behold a golden haired treasure dressed and awaiting his return. She'd gotten ready and had been told by Tommy that the captain had gone to search for Mr. McCray.

With him back she was eager to visit the dressmaker. They'd both decided that he'd go with her. There was so much about clothing in this period that she didn't know. She also didn't want her ignorance caught by any of the local society climbers. She knew only too well how appearances made lasting impressions. Having Daniel close by gave her the confidence she needed.

She met Duncan with a bright smile and McCray understood immediately the pull of this siren. He would have gladly followed her to his death like the old folk stories. Lucky for Daniel she wasn't a siren. He'd have been dead ten times over if she were.

"You did well, sir. She's a definite keeper, but if you decide to throw 'er back let me know where and I'll gladly cast in my line."

Daniel's eyes rested on her laughing countenance. She was mystifying, possessing beauty, intelligence, and kindness, what a catch indeed.

"And where is your dirty mind wandering to, sir?" Brianna asked pretending an injured expression.

"Nowhere dirty, but quite the opposite direction. Your fair beauty astounds me, Bri, my love."

She blushed at his pretty compliment and then said, "My love is it? You certainly are a fine specimen yourself." Winking, she then asked, "Are you ready to visit the dark cave of women's fashion?"

Feigning a wounded look he said, "If I must to appease your unending frivolities."

They both knew the joke in this considering she had no suitable clothes. He'd already requested that her 'past' things be secluded to his enjoyment and knowing the cover up attitude of the era she had easily agreed.

Arriving at Mrs. Delaney's dress shop they found the owner willing to please. It was a rare treat to be allowed to fit such a winsome creature in any amount of fashion. Let alone a whole wardrobe.

The couple was well suited. It was so obvious that the two had a love match. It brought a tear to her eye, it did. Made her miss her deceased husband. He'd been such help around the store. She wished them the best. The gift of love was a precious thing.

Returning to the counter she quickly picked out some lovely bolts of silks and cottons from the bottom cabinet. She reserved these for only her special clients. Most women only wanted strong serviceable clothes or just simple practical cottons. It was a treat for the ladies to exclaim over the colors and textures of the different fabrics.

Daniel watched in wary amusement as his dashing wife charmed the dressmaker. She was a natural friendly person. She listened attentively to the woman as she explained what the fabrics could be used for and then expressed her trust with Mrs. Delaney's judgment.

At such lovely praise the seamstress silently promised herself to make this sweet women the envy of Bridgetown. No, make that the whole island of Barbados.

Stepping into the sunlight as they left the shop both were feeling drained.

"I think I've had my fill of shopping for a long time," Brianna said holding her husband's hand as they walked to the awaiting carriage.

"I have to agree with you. There are so many odds and ends that go with each ensemble. It quite boggles the mind."

"So many choices! Right now I'd love to relax and not worry about more choices."

Assisting Bri up into the carriage and then climbing up himself Daniel was inclined to agree. It'd be so wonderful to get settled.

The carriage driver, Reginald or Reggy by his friends, ambled the large vehicle towards the northeastern end of town. The drive would take approximately three hours, so the occupants eased in for a nice nap.

Reggy pondered the new turn in his life. He was a scraggy fellow with big ears and big arms and a curious earring in one ear. Most wouldn't hire him simply based on his looks, but this Duncan McCray chap hadn't blinked on that. He was more worried about finding good men. At least that's what he'd said at the time of their meeting.

The Mr. and Mrs. seemed like real nice people. Daniel had tipped him extra after leaving the dress shop and had asked that him and his wife be taken to their new home.

It was nice to meet good folks. Reggy was currently an out-of-work buccaneer. None other than Blackbeard himself had shot his captain and after seeing that death, Reggy wanted to live longer. Pirating led to a short life.

There was nothing better than having a good pint and a warm wench. Hopefully now that he had gone respectable, he'd be able to enjoy the two more frequently. He'd never been one of the sea-obsessed types. It saddened him that so many of his cohorts fantasized about the love of the sea. To him it was only a giant pond used for traveling and transportation of goods.

But to each his own he guessed. Besides with the wages he was now receiving he could easily keep both his favorite hobbies and be an asset. It was good to feel the land under his toes, have a nice dry place to sleep, and good money coming in. Plus a fair boss. More often than not the captains he'd worked under were unfeeling and unreasonable.

He'd been told many times that with ears his size it would make sense that he could hear well. Of course that had been when he'd decided not to listen to an order. His captains never understood him to be an asset. He'd always been the dumb one. Insults flew constantly.

He wasn't simple he just liked to stir things up a bit. The daily ship routines became boring and his work ethic almost nonexistent.

So when Captain Rickets was killed, Reggy decided that he'd take a break from sea life and try to make some honest money.

McCray had offered a great job. There wasn't any way that Reggy would have turned it down. Besides, working for Captain Storme on his island home was better than doing the same old ship routine.

Who knows, he thought, there might even be some excitement. And if not he could still while away the hours not working with some good ale and one of the new maids.

A sudden jar in the carriage awoke Brianna. She could feel her excitement building. Daniel and her would endeavor to grow tall and strong together like the palms she now saw passing by her window.

Daniel slept on. She knew he needed the rest. They'd both had a long night and then all that at the dressmakers.

Her new gowns and all that entailed with them would be delivered as they were finished. Luckily, Mrs. Delaney had found three ready-made gowns in her back room. A Mrs. Patience Bonnet had ordered them, but at the last minute had changed her mind. Mrs. Delaney said that's how it went with her. Not that Mrs. Bonnet was disagreeable, but that she was kind of flighty. One day she'd want this and the next that.

"That wouldn't be Mr. Stede Bonnet's wife would it?" Daniel had asked.

"Why yes, sir. Do you happen to know him?"

"Indeed, he did some business with my stepfather for some time. Do they live near here?"

"Yes, sir, I believe they're having a party on Friday. Mrs. Bonnet has ordered a lovely gown."

"Interesting. Well, we might have to drop by. For my stepfather's sake at least."

The idea was intimidating to Brianna. A party with all these old-fashioned people. She'd have to mind her Ps and Qs. She'd have to face the society here soon. Might as well be sooner than later. It was good she had those dresses.

As the carriage crested a fairly large hill she could just make out a white house surrounded by swaying palms. That must be it she thought.

"Daniel, Daniel, wake up," she said gently nudging his sleeping form.

"What is it, Bri?"

"I think we're close. I can see the lawns and the sea," she said, pointing out the window.

"Yes, I believe you're right. The place certainly fits the description I was given. Looks to be in good repair."

They waited as the slow carriage made its ungainly progress in that direction. When they finally arrived in the driveway and came to a stop, Daniel helped Brianna down and the housekeeper, Margaret Bryson, greeted them.

"Margaret, you're looking well. I hope everything's been going good."

Smiling the lady looked inquiringly towards Brianna.

"Of course. How rude of me. Margaret, I'd like you to meet my new wife, Brianna. Bri, this is Margaret Bryson, our housekeeper."

"Lovely to meet you, dear. This boy's been needing to settle down for a long time."

"Thank you Ms. Bryson."

"No, dear. Just call me Margaret. Now come inside and I'll get you a nice glass of cold lemonade."

"That would be wonderful."

"Margaret, has Duncan arrived yet with the wagons?"

"They're out back unloading some of the crates and I'd like to thank you for bringing my trunks. It's been some time since I've had such good things. I mean this is a nice place, but some things are hard to come by and my mother's copper pots are priceless. You've never had better food than what's cooked in them.

Daniel had to agree. Margaret was a wiz in the kitchen. It was one reason they hadn't hired a cook. It was one of her favorite chores and he loved her different culinary treats.

"Bri, Margaret is a wonderful cook. She can take something you really couldn't touch otherwise and make it delectable."

"Now, Danny, don't you be talking like that. You know my cooking is fair. I just like doing it."

"Fair? Now that's putting it mildly" said Daniel grinning.

Everyone had to laugh at that. Margaret had been with Daniel's adopted family for years. She'd started in the kitchens and still preferred that domain. He asked her to come to his new place to be his housekeeper, not only because of her cooking, but because he truly liked her. She was warm and friendly with a sunny disposition, but when her temper flared it was "a cat with its tail caught in the door" like Duncan had said. She could organize a household and still retain a friendliness that instilled motherly trust from the maids.

Currently, Brianna and Margaret were discussing food. Brianna also enjoyed cooking and the group soon had their mouths watering in anticipation.

"I think from both of your expressions that you might like some slices of cake."

"That would be divine," confided Brianna. "I love cake."

"Well then, that's it. I'll get some straight away," she said bustling out to retrieve the tasty morsels.

After their cake and lemonade, Daniel left Brianna, to meet Duncan and go over some affairs of the estate. If a harvest wouldn't be possible, then that'd be fine with Daniel. He was still heavily invested with his stepfather, Richard. The shipping line was doing extremely well. Reliance on the plantation wasn't a big issue. He would like to have a good garden for the house. Any surplus could be traded in Bridgetown for other goods.

"Duncan, what would be your thoughts on the land?"

"Well, sir, to tell the truth she's been depleted mightily. It'll take years to rebuild its strength. I hope that doesn't cause problems."

"No, not at all. You only confirmed my earliest thoughts. What would be your ideas to bring it back to the rich earth it once was?"

"The best first step would be a good turning of the soil. I'll try to introduce some new compounds bit by bit. Hopefully, we'll get everything squared away soon."

"That sounds fine. You do what you think is best."

Duncan noticed the sudden faraway look that came into Daniel's eyes. He could guess where his mind had flown. A certain blonde-haired beauty had bewitched him.

"Well, sir, that's all I've conjured up so far. Not much I know, but it'll be some time before it's enriched again."

"Right. We'll keep thinking and try to work it out slowly. Meanwhile just do what you think will work. I trust your judgment. You've been doing this sort of thing much longer than I."

"If you don't mind my saying, Captain, you might as well high-tail it back to your light-o-love. I'm sure her thoughts are on you too. Being newlyweds and all."

"Thanks for understanding." Daniel said as he realized the redundancy of their conversation. "Have you seen a certain lady yet?"

"She's done forgiven me. Said I was a handful, but that she couldn't help but like my old buzzard's hide."

Margaret did have a way with words when she was riled. Somehow he could picture Duncan ruffling her feathers plenty more in the future.

NINE

The night of the party at the Bonnet's came quickly. Margaret helped Brianna dress and do her hair, being that Brianna had no maid of her own.

Daniel's choice in a bride pleased Margaret to no end. She knew Mr. Richard would be satisfied. The two had similar personalities and what one lacked the other filled. She could only dream of the adorable children the couple would make, full of curiosity and joy.

The cut of Brianna's gown accentuated her womanly curves. It wasn't overly low-cut, but hinted at the delights it contained. Daniel knew she'd be a sensation. There couldn't be a lovelier woman anywhere.

It often hit him at weird moments how dependent he'd become on his new wife. It worried him. He'd never been one of those love-professing dandy's that were so popular these days. In fact the only woman he recalled loving was his mother. Could these feelings he had for his delectable spouse be love?

Margaret had seen them off in the carriage. The drive

wouldn't take long. The Bonnet's home was only two hours away. He had ample time to consider his confused thoughts and to gaze upon the object of his rambling mind. What was she thinking?

Brianna's mind was a whirl. Her past could have never prepared her for a moment like this. She only hoped she didn't say anything wrong or make some sort of blunder. If she listened instead of talking a lot she'd learn what these islanders were like. Funny, but she felt she was approaching an unknown battlefield.

Surely a simple party wouldn't be that bad. Somehow that didn't help to calm the butterflies dancing madly about in her stomach.

"Is everything all right, dear? You've turned a shade of green," Daniel felt compelled to ask, noticing the panicked look that had crossed Brianna's features.

"Yes, I'm just a bit nervous. I've never been to a party like this," she said trying to calm down.

Seeing now the course of her worry, he wanted to sooth her in some way.

"Don't worry so much, these people are just that, people. You'll do just fine," he said, reaching over to clasp her hand.

"Besides, I'll be right there to help you through. I can remember the last time I saw Stede. He'd arrived to see Richard, to order some crates of bananas, and we got on famously," he said, giving her hand a squeeze. "He'd mentioned his wife and how he worried about her temperament. Seems she's a bit of a hellion at times. Poor Stede, he's quite taken with her though. Said her good qualities outweighed the bad."

Just the sound of Daniel's voice relaxed the tension that

had been building within her. The rolling quality of it as he continued to talk of Stede and his mysterious wife eased the tightened coil in her belly. In fact, it caused chills to spread across her skin like soft waves on the shore line as his voice both suppressed the negative feelings and let loose a crazy desire to kiss his sweet lips.

Such a strong pull between them it was amazing that less than a week ago she'd worried about money and work. Now she was married and secure with a man who was handsome, strong, and intelligent.

Daniel finished his story and noted the difference in Brianna. She had calmed considerably. She reminded him of a high-strung mare. All fire and get-up, but once you tamed her you could use the smallest assurances and she trusted you completely. He'd never considered how having the trust of a woman would feel, but now he knew it was indeed a heady drug. This woman's trust meant a great deal to him and he'd do this best to keep it in tact.

"Is it much further?" she asked looking at the unending visage of palms, vines, and bananas trees.

"Shouldn't be. By my calculations about thirty minutes or so. Are you still worried?"

"Not near as much. Like you said, they're people. I've worked in offices before and the employees could be very catty, always gossiping and trying to fit into different cliques. I'll just pretend it's like that."

"It doesn't appear to me that you enjoyed your workplace much," he remarked noting her lack of enthusiasm.

"Oh, the work wasn't bad, just all the drama that came with it. I've never been one to fall into the crowd and nod yes to what the group leader was saying. We called these people 'yes' men. They made the self-appointed leaders feel important. You know, to have these leeches following them around telling them, 'of course sir,' and 'that's right, no problem.' I guess I'd rather sit back in a corner and get my job done."

"I'm certainly glad you're here now and you definitely don't have to agree with me on everything to make me feel bigger. Just to have you on my arm as we walk through town makes my ego soar!" He grinned wickedly and leaned over to pinch her leg through her dress. "Besides, I respect your intelligence and would rather you state your mind than hide away."

Brianna sighed and leaned against his shoulder. She could only ponder what else this twisted fate had in store for her. What next?

The carriage began to roll down the cobbled drive. They both noticed the lovely gardens surrounding the home. The Chinese lanterns swung gently in the breeze beneath the warm glow emanating from the many windows of the house.

Reggy brought the carriage to a halt and alighted to help the Mrs. down. She was certainly a sight for his old sea eyes and Mr. Storme cut a nice figure himself.

"Thank you, Reggy. Feel free to get some refreshments in the kitchen. Sounds like they're enjoying the party, too."

The sounds of happy revelry could be heard from inside the house and around back at the kitchen. It looked to be a lovely evening.

As they ascended, the steps leading to the door, it opened and a portly man in a black suit appeared.

"Can I help you, sir?"

"Yes, we're here to visit Stede. I hope he doesn't mind our unannounced arrival at his party."

"Your name, sir?"

Brianna couldn't believe it but the man reminded her of Lurch from *The Addams Family*, although on a much smaller scale. He was quite grizzly in appearance and not very vocal. She'd have to tell Daniel later. He'd enjoy the joke.

"Mr. And Mrs. Daniel Storme."

"Thank you, sir. If you'll wait here, I'll inform Mr. Bonnet of your presence."

Watching the scowling butler as he turned on his errand, Brianna could barely stifle the giggle from escaping. Daniel turned to her eyebrows quirked in question and she had to whisper, "I'll tell you later."

No telling what had touched his wife's warped sense of humor.

"Daniel. Daniel Storme. Look at you," spoke a handsome man dressed to the nines. "Appearing on my doorstep and with a beautiful bride in tow."

"It's nice to see you, Stede," Daniel said extending his hand. "This is my wife, Brianna."

"Lovely, my girl. Your name suits you."

Reaching behind him he pulled the arm of a lovely lady dressed in scarlet red and dripping diamonds from her ears and neck.

"This is my wife, Patience. My wonderful Patty."

"Stede, who are these people?" the lady in red asked eyeing him with distant interest.

"Oh Daniel's the son of my good colleague, Richard Smithfield in Nassau. You remember, dear?"

"Yes, the name is familiar. So you decided to visit now?" she asked with a lift of her brows.

"We heard of your party in Bridgetown at the dressmakers. She was kind enough to fill in the details for us and I couldn't wait to surprise Stede."

Brianna could tell by this exchange that Mrs. Bonnet just might have a bee buzzing around in her head. She was indeed a mystery. Dressed in scarlet and wearing many jewels you'd think she was a fancy girl making her success known.

The lady's gaze never wavered from Brianna quizzical stare and before her careful husband took notice she said, "I can see you're no wimpy, ninny hammer ready to run at the first sight of an insect, Mrs. Storme. Do come inside and I'll introduce you around."

With that backwards complement, Brianna felt compelled to go. Maybe it wasn't a bee, but a hornet she thought. This woman would put any general to shame. To be her size, which was maybe five feet two inches and willowy slim, she was certainly a handful. No wonder Mr. Bonnet had that worried look. You never knew what his Patty was going to say.

Brianna knew Stede had to be in his fifties, but his indomitable bride could be anywhere from thirty-five to forty. She definitely was fiery and the dress suited her temper. Only time would prove to her if the dragon were a friend or foe.

"Johnny, I'd like to introduce you to Mrs. Brianna

Storme. She and her husband just arrived and decided to drop by."

"Nice to meet you, Mrs. Storme."

"Johnny's our local reverend," she said as they continued to stroll.

The guests at the party were all friendly. Some even knew of Daniel's stepfather. Congratulations were offered to her on the recent marriage and a handful of ladies invited her to tea.

As the two stunning ladies wandered through the crowd Daniel and Stede enjoyed a glass of fine port. Watching Daniel's eyes follow the lovely figure of his wife, Stede understood the hunger written across his features.

He also loved his wife immensely. She was a spitfire and terribly blunt at times, but she was also loving, loyal, and oh so wonderful to gaze upon. If the young couple were blessed with half the excitement that him and Patty enjoyed, then they'd indeed be happy.

"How's things been in Bridgetown?" Daniel asked pulling his eyes off the ladies.

"Fair," he said taking a sip of his port, "with Jamaica beginning to grow sugar cane, the markets not been what it used to be. I sure hope being as you bought the old Parker place that you're not going to pursue that course."

"No, I've seen how everyone's been struggling with the prices and the losses in production. I'm looking into a few prospects, but I think for now, I'll stick to the things I know."

"Mainly shipping much needed products," Stede commented. "Richard always knew that when people develop their needs grow also. I'm glad to see you follow in his footsteps."

"The only problem with that, Stede, is he has mighty big feet."

The two gentlemen enjoyed the laugh, both knowing that Richard did indeed have large feet. His cobbler was amazed and often joked that a pair of boots for Mr. Smithfield used a whole cow.

Brianna was surprised to note that she was having a good time. Although she missed being with Daniel, she could see him drinking with Stede. Patty, as she insisted she be called, had turned out to be a hoot. She knew everyone here and all the gossip in between. Her tidbits about the Dyer's dog next door had been hilarious.

Evidently the mutt had worked its way over from their plantation. The Dyers were Patty and Stede's nearest neighbors. Well, the dog had arrived to visit covered in leaves and some sticky substance. He was acting funny so the servants had gotten Patty.

As it turned out, Tiny, a Great Dane and chow mix, had found to his sweet tooth delight: a beehive full of honey. As the silly boy gorged himself on the sticky treat, he didn't notice the flying swarm of bees that he'd mightily offended. The swarm had begun their onslaught and the spooked animal took off on a run through the various vines and vegetation.

The yummy honey-glue helped form a coating of leaves around his body protecting everything but his ears. Tiny enjoyed rolling in his food, like most dogs. By the time Tiny had ran the whole way to Patty's home, the bee's had given up on the chase, deciding is was easier to rebuild their now destroyed structure. His ears were swollen to the size of pears.

Mary, Patty's cook, had been picking vegetables in the

garden when this large camouflaged monster arrived barking all the way. Because of the leaves and honey combo and the swollen area between his ears, poor Tiny resembled a long legged watermelon plant on the rampage. Miss Mary, needless to say, screamed and fainted dead away.

She swore she'd never be able to eat another watermelon without the thought of it now eating her. After the discovery that is was the loveable Tiny, incognito, it still didn't relieve Mary's new fear. Brianna still snickered in remembrance.

The night wore on. Dinner was called around nine o'clock and she happily took her place beside Daniel. He noticed her happy glow and how everyone was treating her with obvious envy and respect.

Patty had really helped smooth things over. Currently residing at the head of the table she pondered on the island's newest arrivals. They made a handsome couple. For some odd reason she felt drawn to Brianna. The girl appeared innocent. She was intelligent, but seemed to lack something. It still boggled in her mind exactly what that something was. The girl was different, but not noticeably unless you really paid attention.

It wasn't her southern accent or her appearance. What could it be? She'd have the girl over for lunch and she could observe her at her leisure. Patty would contain her curiosity for now and focus on the party, which was now at a crucial point and starting the dinner of six courses. She needed to be on at her best. You never know when something terrible could happen.

After saying their goodbyes to the Bonnet's, the two climbed wearily into the carriage for the ride home.

The night had gone well. He'd known Brianna would be fine even with all the differences she had to deal with.

She'd filled him in on all her funny comparisons and on the things she noticed, like Lurch the butler. She also told him of the story about Tiny. They both laughed, but were soon tired.

The long day had finally finished. It wasn't long after her colorful stories that Brianna started nodding off in the seat.

Daniel carefully laid her head on his shoulder. He was tired too. All the things him and Stede had discussed rolled through his mind, plants, stocks, the complications of shipping, and more sensitive crops.

Daniel's impressions of Stede were still improving. Richard had always said that not only was Stede uppercut, but he also had a sharp grasp of business. Stede's advice had been simple.

"Don't pursue the growing, son. Try to expand your shipping line within Bridgetown Harbor. There's always going to be a need for supplies and someone to haul the crops to and fro. If you are careful in your planning and gathered in a few choice investors, you could even branch off from Richard and take a chance on your own fleet."

Daniel now pondered the thought, his own fleet. It did have a nice ring to it. Tomorrow he'd broach the subject with Brianna and see what she thought.

Back in the harbor, at the Sea Gull Tavern, known for it's low-class cliental, Lefty Shakes, former pirate captain extraordinaire, plotted his sweet revenge. He'd spread around talk of his needing men ruthless and violent. He'd discussed barter with a man deep into his cups looking to trade rum for his ship. The man had given up hope on life and had squandered his life away on the delightful taste of Caribbean rum.

Lefty, after filling the man's belly with the sweet fiery liquid, had gotten the ship for a mere pittance. A drunken man made for an easily taken in fool. He sneered a lopsided half smile as he contemplated his latest accomplishment.

So far, a crew of Bridgetown's nastiest was easy to accumulate. He'd only need a few more men before he could put step two into action.

"Barney, get your sorry hide over here," Lefty barked to a dumpy looking man with pockmarked skin.

"Yes, Cap'n. What you be needin' sir?"

"You said something about that Storme fellow having a new bride and that she was easy on the eyes."

"Yes, sir. That I did. She wore plum purty and all. I see'd her myself as they got into their carriage."

"Well that's fine news indeed, that'll make my plans much more interesting. Barney, fetch Rawlings and Slick. I've got orders for them I'm sure they'll enjoy."

"Yes, sir. I'll be on my way then. They're just out back. Rawlings said he thought you might want him close, just in case."

"Good. It's nice to find cutthroats with a little brains left."

Barney disappeared out the back door and returned promptly with Rawlings and Slick tailing behind.

Rawlings was a typical pirate. Dirty, unshaven and willing to go to the highest bidder. Slick was his shadow, a man that looked like the name he was called by. In fact, he made it a daily routine of grooming his long black hair back with thick handfuls of lard. Neither man noticed the awful smell that accompanied their persons. Nor did they really care.

"Rawlings, just the nasty person I wanted to see," Lefty said gesturing towards a couple chairs.

"Pull up a seat and I'll tell you what I need."

Lefty wanted no chance of being overheard and leaned forward to tell the intrigued Rawlings the plan. Slick waited patiently knowing he'd eventually be told the plot. He preferred to let Rawlings do the thinking. It left him free to pursue his other favorite pleasures: drinking and women.

Rawlings face lit up with an evil glint as Lefty filled him in. He didn't much like this snake Lefty, but the money was good and he didn't care what deeds he and Slick did. You couldn't find many jobs like this one. Lefty would pay him well to pull this off. Besides, how much trouble could one woman be?

TEN

It was now a week since Daniel and Brianna had visited the Bonnets. This morning Brianna had a message asking if she'd like to go on a short shopping expedition into Bridgetown with Patty Bonnet.

She must've made a good impression. Mrs. Bonnet said she'd be by around eleven o'clock this morning to pick her up. They'd drive in her carriage and enjoy the coolness of the morning.

Brianna couldn't help but wonder if this was a friendly call or a search for gossip. She still felt on edge with these old-fashioned people. Although now she guessed she'd have to start conforming more to this period. It was just such a hard transition.

She was used to women's rights and such. It was so much more confining now. There was no way she was going to get used to corsets. Besides her waist was small enough already. She wasn't *Barbie* and she wasn't going to force her body to look like one either.

Daniel had already told her not to worry about corsets. He didn't care a fig about fashion as long as she was happy.

The outing would be very different. Recently, she'd shopped with Daniel and he'd handled most of the choices, knowing that she wouldn't have a clue. How then would she fool Mrs. Bonnet?

Sighing, she finished her toilet and checked her watch. Almost time for her guest, in fact, she thought she could hear the gravel in the drive as a carriage approached.

She arrived down stairs in time to hear the voices of Mrs. Bonnet and Margaret talking.

"How lovely to see you again, Mrs. Bonnet," Brianna said.

"It's still Patty, dear," she said smiling. "Shall we be off? I know I'm early but I like to get out and beat the heat before it's to overbearing."

"Yes, let's go then. Tell Daniel to expect me late this evening."

"Yes, Ms. Brianna. I'll see that he knows."

Once the ladies were seated, they started the drive to town.

"I don't go into town very often, you know. It's such a ways and I'm not as young as I used to be."

"You're not that old, Patty."

"Thank you. You are a dear, but yes, I'll be turning forty this year."

"That's not that old."

"Well, I guess it's not really, is it?" she looked at the confused Brianna and winked. "It's just something you say, I guess."

Brianna thought that Patty certainly was quirky. One minute she seemed to care about society and the next not to care one whit.

"I know I'm rather contrary," Patty continued, "but I just can't help it. You see, it's my nature. I like to stir things up a bit. Just when Steddy thinks I'll do one thing, I turn it around and mix it up good. Keeps him on his toes. That way he doesn't grow old to fast."

"Makes sense, I guess," said Brianna.

Patty nodded her head, "You're quite a mix yourself, Brianna. I've watched you and there's a piece of your puzzle that doesn't quite fit."

Seeing the fear that popped into Briannas' eyes, Patty knew she'd hit a nerve. It looked to be a big one at that.

"I know I shouldn't pry, but like I said earlier, with my contrary nature I often do things I shouldn't. If you'd like to talk, I'll gladly listen."

This woman appeared sincere, but you never knew. Besides, spilling the beans wouldn't do anyone any good.

"I really don't know what you mean, Patty?"

"Well that's fine then. I just thought I'd ask. I understand how one's past isn't really something you want public. Just remember if you ever need to talk I'll be around."

"Thanks anyways, Patty."

"So to change this serious subject, what do you need from town?"

"Well I just ordered some things from the dress shops. So not clothes."

"Then let's re-word the question. What do you want from town, dear?"

As Brianna considered this she thought she might like to get Daniel a gift. He'd given her a handful of coins before he left out this morning for his meeting with Duncan. She guessed she had plenty to find him something nice.

"Maybe a book. I'd like to get Daniel something."

Patty smiled at the response Brianna had given. Nothing like newlyweds to make you feel old.

Overall the trip to town wasn't bad. Both ladies felt a bond that drew them closer. Soon, Brianna was telling some tidbits about her past and so was the ever-changing Patty.

"I suppose you think I was born to money," Patty commented.

"I really had no clue either way," Brianna said.

"Surprising as it might be, I wasn't. Most around here don't know because I've chose for them not to, but I'll tell you."

Patty was born in a small village in England. She'd been the youngest of seven children, four boys and three girls. When she was old enough, her sisters taught her things a lady should know.

Especially her sister Kitty, she was a maid up at the big house. She'd often told the small Patty stories that were gossiped about in the servants' hall.

The lord and the lady of the house had a son named Rupert. Rupert wasn't the smartest lad, but because his parents were wealthy, he could do no wrong. The young maids were all leery of him. He was known to be a handsy, spoiled boy, and they all were glad when he left again for school.

Christmas fast approached and everyone up at the big house was getting ready for the festivities.

Young Rupert arrived home with a handsome friend in tow. His friend's name was Stede Bonnet. He also came from a well-to-do family, but unlike Rupert, he was a gentleman.

Kitty had brought young Patty, who was around fifteen at the time, up with her to help with the festivities.

Patty was ripe for the plucking, or so Mr. Rupert thought. He cornered poor Patty in the downstairs linen closet and told her to keep her mouth shut or she'd face the consequences. Patty stared in wide-eyed fear as the young man began undoing the buttons of his clothes.

As he reached to push her down, she screamed. Stede had been looking for Rupert and at the scream snatched open the door.

Rupert fumbled with his clothes.

"What's going on here, Rupert? I didn't know you liked to terrorize your help?"

"The girl teased me and I thought to teach her a lesson."

Stede had never seen this side of Rupert and it made him sick. The sight of the poor girls tears brought him around.

He held out his hand and she gazed at him in adoration. A true knight, she thought in her head.

"I've not finished with that one yet! Where are you taking her?"

Stede was nine years older than the young Patty, but it didn't matter.

"I'm taking her home."

"No you're not! You're my guest, in my home. You'll do as I say!"

"'Fraid not old, boy. I'm two years your senior and only came visiting because you begged me. Guess I don't care for your bullying nature. Odd that only now does so much makes sense."

"What do you mean?"

"Well, at school you were very persuasive and cunning, but now I see it's your raising."

"If you leave with her, I'll spread it about that you carried her off for rape."

Glancing behind him, Stede noticed how Patty looked at him with trust. Rupert glared in obvious annoyance.

"I think not. Besides, I think I'll marry the girl. She looks intelligent and in need of a hero."

"If you do you'll be ostracized from society!"

"I don't give a fig for society. My parents want me to marry before I leave England and I've chosen. Thank you for your Christmas invitation. Sorry, but I've much to do now."

Rupert felt he'd been bested. The wench didn't deserve all the luck of what marrying into one of Virginia's best families would entail. He'd be more careful from now on not to invite any more of the visiting colonials to his home. They were far too rude for his taste. He'd only wanted a quick tumble after all.

Stede helped Patty home and discussed the marriage details with her family.

He offered her father a nice settlement so that her family wouldn't be left out to the likes of Rupert.

Her parents were glad to see their youngest go and to be married to such a catch. They didn't dwell on the "whys." They just knew that little Patty would have it much better than them.

Stede considered Patty a means to an end. He knew his family wouldn't care for him marrying a commoner, but he didn't care. He didn't see the class system succeeding forever. People were all people. Good or bad.

As the two of them grew together, the bond between them had grown. Now after twenty-five years of marriage, they were deeply in love. At the time Stede had not known how complex Patty was, but now he'd come to really love her ways.

He was fond of saying, "That woman keeps my blood boiling and keeps me young."

Their tempers were both crazy, but so was their love.

After Patty had finished this detailed monologue, Brianna felt a little sad that she couldn't share more of herself, but Patty understood. Things took time.

You never know how special the bond between people is until you experience it yourself, thought Brianna.

The carriage pulled into town just shy of one o'clock and the two decided to have a late lunch at the restaurant in the hotel lobby. Neither noticed the slimy pair that rubbed their hands in glee at their arrival.

"Which one is it?" asked Slick.

"The blonde, but the brunette ain't half bad neither. We'll have to take them both. Can't have no witnesses and I'd hate to kill that older one."

"Me too! Reckon old Lefty will let us keep her?"

"Well what he don't know won't hurt him, the way I figure."

"I'm glad you think well, Rawlings. Things get to complicated and it makes me brain hurt."

"I know Slick. Don't waste your brain on it. I'll handle everything."

Slick just nodded in agreement and the two set in wait next to the dress shop. They also had a good view of the hotel from here.

Rising from their table, Patty remarked, "Brianna, you could do with a nice hat. You're skin's very nice, you really don't need to burn."

"Do you know of anyplace that would have something nice?"

"Yes, in fact, the dress shop across the way has a wonderful selection. I think something wide-brimmed, maybe in green."

"I trust you, Patty. My taste is rather odd."

This statement raised one of Patty's expressive brows, but she made no comment. One thing she'd noticed about Brianna was she listened closely and tended to brush off decisions which most women would have had made firm choices. Almost like she was taking notes and learning things anew. Patty understood. It'd taken her years to learn all she had about society. It was indeed an evil web. Being careful was one of the best ways to succeed.

Slick elbowed Rawlings, as the two women eased their way down the boardwalk toward Mrs. Delaney's Dress Emporium.

They didn't notice the two miscreants hiding between the buildings in the alley, which worked out well for the villains.

Rawlings gave the signal and the two reached out and grabbed the ladies arms. Both were pulled into the alley and gags quickly put into place.

"Good you thought of the gags. These two are both spit-fires," Slick said eying the simmering ladies in satisfaction.

"Once we deliver the blonde, we can really enjoy this fancy piece," Rawlings said, rubbing Patty's cheek.

Brianna and Patty were concealed underneath potato sacks and thrown over the shoulders of the men. As they were carried toward the docks, they noticed the sounds of the harbor.

Why would these two goons abduct her and Patty? She didn't know anyone here. What could be the motive?

The Sea Gull Tavern had seen many illegal plots carried out. The patrons and the employees kept their eyes and ears shut. The quickest way to die was to be a snitch.

The sight of two large potato sacks and the bearers of such were no new thing and were paid no mind.

Lefty eyed their arrival with true joy. Step two was finished, but wait. Why were there two sacks?

"Who's trussed up in the other, Slick?" Lefty asked, giving Rawlings a fearful look. Rawlings took the cue.

"Ah, don't worry about that any, Cap'n Lefty. It's just some woman that the other was with. We thought we'd keep her for some fun."

"Who might the lady be?"

"Don't know. Didn't ask her 'fore we trussed her up," Rawlings declared. "Didn't think you'd care being as we got the one you wanted and all."

"Well, great," Lefty muttered. "Take them both to the back room and we'll get this settled."

Rawlings still had no love for Lefty, but for the sake of curiosity he did as he was told.

Dumping their burdens unceremoniously onto the floor of the nicest room the Sea Gull could offer and stepping back to watch the bugs scatter, Lefty lit the lamp and the sacks were removed.

Barney hadn't lied. The blonde was indeed a sight and he could see why his cutthroats were taken with the other. The eyes staring above the gags glared in annoyance. Fighters, both of them.

"Well, boys, you did good. Real good. From the looks of this one's clothes we've got a real hob knobber on our hands," pointing to Patty. "A bonus ransom is indeed nice."

Rawlings felt a jolt. He'd wanted that one, but if she were rich, the gold would do nicely.

"Remove her gag and let's see who she is."

"What do you filthy toad-mongers want," rasped Patty as she got the saliva working in her mouth again.

"Well, pretty lady, first off, what's your name?"

"I'm Patricia Bonnet and my husband's Stede Bonnet. He'll make you pay dearly for this!"

"Such fire," Lefty said, rubbing his scar, wishing life would again reach where it had been severed. One such as this would be joy to tame.

"Old Stede Bonnet's wife, eh? That old coot has plenty of money. I'm sure he'd pay dearly to get you back."

"So you kidnapped us for ransom?"

"Not necessarily dear, your friend here, Mrs. Storme, is going to help me repay a long standing debt."

Brianna wished she weren't gagged. She'd try to keep this creepy old man talking. He had that braggart's way about him. She hoped Patty picked that up too.

"What kind of debt?"

"Young Storme should've died years ago. His father died

and his cheap mother. I made sure of that. Some how that young boy escaped my wrath."

"What happened for you to kill them?" Patty inquired. She had also noticed this man's urge to talk. Revenge seemed to seep from his pores or maybe that was only the smell of the greasy looking black haired man. "I mean, why go to the trouble?"

"Good question," he said rubbing his chin. "If I were able, I'd teach you a thing or two, but thanks to that no good Hammock it's just not possible," he said with a wicked sneer. "Hammock thought he could leave my crew, the only way to leave my crew is death. So he had to die. During our fight I suffered a severe injury to my manhood. To get even I plan to finish the job I started. I'll kill that brat yet!" Lefty finished his rampage and wiped the spittle from his lips. Just thinking about it all, made his anger fly into a frenzy.

"Gag her again. She asks to many questions," Lefty snarled, "You two follow me. I'll get your pay and I'll tell you our next move."

The lamp left with the trio of villains. They could hear the grating voice of the one called Lefty as he gave them orders for the night.

Brianna thought that it looked like she and Patty would be staying here a while. She just hoped the bugs didn't come out.

Soon she heard the hurried traffic of the six-legged vermin. Oh she hated creepy-crawlies.

This whole situation had her mind spinning. In the dim interior of their room she could barely make out the figure of Patty as she leaned against the wall. Somehow she'd have to get some rest too.

If only the goons had undone their wrists. At least they hadn't tied their ankles. Maybe she could wiggle her hand free. It'd be wonderful to get these hateful ropes off.

Working diligently on the knots with her thumbs, she slowly eased some of the tension. Her mind went over everything Lefty had said.

So he'd killed Daniel's mom and dad. The whole mess sounded very *Godfather*-like. The only way out of that family had been death. Sad way to live, she thought. Funny, that the mean old man couldn't use the part that made him a man. Somehow that seemed like poetic justice to her.

Her panic rose and fell as she thought. Like a roller coaster, her emotions moved. One of the most important things she knew was she wouldn't give up. She'd not let this villain defeat her newfound love in her newfound life. She would survive, somehow.

ELEVEN

Dusk had just fallen and Daniel was worried. It wasn't like Brianna to be late and he'd just received a message from Stede asking if Patty was still at the Stormes' home.

He'd informed the boy to tell Stede that he'd neither one of the ladies. His mind ran rampant at what could be holding them up. Maybe the carriage had lost a wheel or maybe they'd stayed in town for an early dinner

He knew one thing, whenever he got his hands on Brianna he was going to hug her so close and then wring her neck. All in all he knew this just wasn't like his bride.

As the hours passed by and still no Brianna, he decided to head into town himself. Surely someone would know the whereabouts of the two women.

He sent a message with Duncan to Stede Bonnet telling him his plan to go into Bridgetown and look for clues. He couldn't think of anyone that would do them harm, but in a harbor like Bridgetown with the taverns and lowlifes that frequented them, who knew.

They'd only been here a short time and already their bliss

had been interrupted. He'd just stick to the hope that he'd meet the carriage on the way there.

He arrived in town close to nine o'clock. Going down the main road he noticed the closed dress shop and the hotel. He guessed he'd get a room and then ask around.

Two such lovely ladies wouldn't go unnoticed.

Brianna awoke with a start. She didn't recall nodding off, but realized it was now dark.

The noises of the tavern were just starting to liven up. Amazing how your other senses magnified when one was restricted. Her wrists were cramped and cold from the lack of circulation. It would be nice if she could talk, then she'd know exactly where Patty was located.

She scooted around using her legs as feelers, until she bumped into what must be a table. She grunted and continued her wormlike movements until she heard a return mumble of words.

If they could sit closer together maybe the knots she'd fiddled with earlier would come undone. They were both lucky the goons had tied their hands in the front. Brianna couldn't imagine the pain of having them bound behind her back for so long.

As she wiggled her fingers across the fabric of Patty's dress, she worked her fingers up to the gag in Patty's mouth leaning back with her waiting to pull it out.

"Oh, how glorious to move my mouth again," Patty said working her jaws open and shut to relieve the tight muscles.

"Here let me get yours and we'll try to shed some light on this mess."

With that said, Patty wiggled her bound wrists around until she felt Brianna's nose with her finger tips. Using the ends of her nails she gripped on and pulled.

"One never knows the joy of freedom until someone takes it away."

"Amen!" commented Patty.

"Now that we can talk what's your opinion on the mess?"

"I think that nasty old man has a few bats in his belfry. Stede will not sit idle while some greasy weasel holds me prisoner."

"Nor will Daniel. Especially when he finds out that this man was responsible for such a loss in his life."

"Patty, do you think if we sit close together that we could undo these stupid ropes?"

"Say no more, Brianna, let's at least try."

They both scooted around, reaching out blindly in the blackness. Once their hands met the two sat quietly as each took a try at the tangled knots. Slowly, Patty began pulling one long end. "This darkness certainly doesn't help," she said.

Considering neither could see a clock, they had no idea how long their fumbling took. It seemed like hours, although in this ink, dark time stood still.

Once the final strand was pulled off Brianna started working on Patty's.

"I wonder what time it is?"

At Patty's question, she remembered she'd worn her Indiglo watch. Pushing the side, the little face lit up. Patty looked on in amazement. "I've never seen anything like that. What is it?"

"Just my watch," she said. Her mind quickly registered the Indiglo was not standard in 1717. How would she explain that to Patty without losing her new friend?

"I've never seen a watch do that. Where did you get it? It's very clever."

From the tone of voice, Patty didn't sound freaked out. Maybe she'd forget she had seen it.

"Oh, yeah, by the way its almost ten o'clock."

"Could you show me the light again? Somehow it seems to lift my spirits.

"Sure, I guess," Brianna said, pushing the little button again.

"Well dear, I said before I won't pry until your ready, but that is certainly a special watch," Patty said wondering where and how such a device could be created.

"It's okay, Patty. We've got some time to waste until the jerks come back, unless the door isn't locked," she felt the wall behind her and moved her hands up the sides until she felt the knob. "It's locked. Oh well, it was worth a shot."

In this long speech, Brianna had displayed more strange English than Patty could keep up with.

"I guess I'll start at the beginning."

"Are you sure, Brianna? You don't have to explain anything, dear. I can tell you're a good person."

"Like I said before, Patty, it's okay. If we're going to be good friends and I'd really like that, then I'd like to be truthful with you."

The two sat propped against the wall and talked the

night away. Brianna explained things as best she could, both trying to focus on her story and not their strange plight.

"Rise and shine my pretty ladies. It's time to get up!"

Brianna and Patty were startled awake from the stale voice of Slick.

"Cap'n Lefty, said you was to take care of your needs in this here pot and then we'd be on our way." He said this as he slid a crusty looking chamber pot their way.

The light from the hall was just enough for them to see that at least the filthy encrusted pot was empty.

"If you'd kindly shut the door, we'll take care of what you ask," said Patty stretching her legs to stand.

"Fine, Miss High and Mighty, you get five minutes!" He shut the door with a slam, disappointed that he wouldn't get to see any of their lovely backsides.

"Brianna, what time is it?"

"Almost four thirty. I guess we'll be on the move, soon. I wonder if there's any way we could leave a clue in case someone looks here."

"That's a good idea. I know," Patty said as she pulled some lace off her collar. "I'll put this on the table near that rag. Then, who knows, maybe Stede or Daniel will get to this point. I make my own lace and Stede would know the design anywhere."

About the time she'd hidden the piece and Brianna finished her turn on the pot the door opened and their smelly guide drew them outside and down the passage.

"Looks like you worked out of your ropes. Ole Lefty won't like that. Said you was to smart and uppity to chance it. Gimme your hands."

Both looked as though they'd like to throttle this varmit.

It was then that Rawlings took the moment to show his flea-bitten self.

"Ahoy, ladies. Did you rest well?" he said.

The two ladies scowled in anger neither wishing to comment at his pleasant attitude.

"Slick, where's their ropes?" he asked ignoring the women.

"Must've took them off last night. Clever, they are."

"Well, no matter," two potato sacks were produced and more dreaded rope, but this time instead of tying their wrists the one named Slick proved his name.

"Lookee here, Rawlings. Once we put these here sacks over their bodies we can wrap this rope around the sacks, keep 'em from squirming so much."

"Good idea, Slick. That'll hold 'em good."

Brianna and Patty were now trussed up like Christmas turkeys. The gags hadn't been replaced. They'd discussed last night various ways to escape, but without a weapon they had decided to wait on a better chance.

"Slick, Rawlings, hurry quickly we're almost fully loaded and ready to cast off."

"Yes, sir, Cap'n Lefty."

As the small group trailed up the gangplank the order was given and the ship pulled anchor and set sail.

"Stupid sacks," thought Brianna. "We can't even see which direction we're leaving."

"Take the women below deck. I'll deal with them later. Remember to post guard. I'll not have them harmed yet."

"Yes, Cap'n."

Daniel's search was proving a challenge. The hotel clerk had said that the lovely Mrs. Bonnet and her friend had lunch in the lobby restaurant. He'd overheard them talking about hats as they left. Other than these small fragments of conversation the man had no thought has to where they'd went.

It was too late to bother Mrs. Delaney at the dress shop, but this wasn't a normal day. His wonderful bride Brianna was missing.

His stride was purposeful as he left the hotel lobby. He'd bang on the door until he woke the town.

Knocking loudly on the door, the door he knew that led to Mrs. Delaney's apartment, he waited.

"Mr. Storme. This is quite a surprise. Is everything all right?"

"No, Mrs. Delaney it is not. My wife and Mrs. Stede Bonnet are missing. They came into town today to do some shopping, but never came home."

"Oh dear," she said. "Do come in. Tell me what you know and I'll try to help. I did see the ladies out walking, but not after lunch. I assumed they'd visit my shop. Mrs. Bonnet is fond of my straw hats."

"Yes, the hotel clerks had mentioned something about hats," he sighed and brushed his fingers through his hair.

The gesture showed how upset this nice man was.

"Did you see anything strange today, Mrs. Delaney, or maybe some strange persons?"

"Well, no I don't think so. Wait! Now that I recall there was a couple of odd characters in the area this morning. An old man and two nasty looking men."

"Do you remember anything else?"

"Yes, in fact the men were talking animatedly and one said,

'Whenever you see her in town alert me and I'll...' oh what was it? Oh yes, he said, 'Alert me and I'll ready the ship.'"

Could this be a coincidence or a plotted scheme? And who were they after? He didn't know of any enemies he had. He wondered if they'd been after Stede's wife and had taken both because they were together.

After leaving Mrs. Delaney, Daniel's mind wondered what had happened to Patty's carriage and the driver. Surely the man would have notified Stede when he couldn't find Mrs. Bonnet, but the message from Stede hadn't mentioned anything to do with the man or the vehicle for that matter, Daniel wandered through town looking for some sign of his wife. He could feel her presence and knew she still lived. He'd go back to the hotel and await word from Stede. In the morning, surely things would look better.

Stede was in fact on his way to town, close behind Daniel.

The waiting was driving him crazy. His darling Patty was always early. Punctuality was one of her best traits.

The woman could truly be a thorn in his side sometimes, but he did love her dearly.

The carriage had never come home. He figured if anything, Scotty, their driver, would have arrived with worry or news. No one had.

Now Bridgetown called him. His Patty was in some sort of trouble.

He accomplished the ride in record time arriving at the hotel in time to meet Daniel who'd just gotten back from his walk and interview with Mrs. Delaney.

"Any news, son?" Stede asked.

"No, sir. I wish there were. I just don't see how two well-dressed women could disappear like this."

"Have you seen my carriage and driver?"

"I've looked around, but it's hard to see anything. I did have a talk with Mrs. Delaney at the dress store. She said she'd seen some men skulking about. She gave me descriptions, but again I'll have to wait until morning.

"That's probably best for both of us. Not that we'll sleep or anything. Would you join me for a drink?

"Sounds good, a whiskey would do me wonders."

The men drank late into the night. They weren't drinking to get drunk, but to soothe their worried nerves. Together they might come to a solution.

Dawn the next morning showed both men were talking in low tones over breakfast.

"Daniel, you visit the livery and see if my carriage showed up. I'll set off to the oceanfront taverns. Maybe someone saw something."

"That's as good a plan as any. Shall we meet up here for dinner and discuss what we've found?"

"Fine then. I'm off. See you later and good luck."

"Good luck to you too, son, I'm afraid we'll need it."

Daniel asked to see the man in charge at the livery.

"Name's Paul, sir. What can I do for you?"

"I'm looking for a carriage. Stede Bonnet's in fact, his driver also. His and my wife came to town yesterday and are missing now."

"Well, sir, I did see Scotty drive through town, but he

didn't drop by as usual. The missus gave him a couple hours to enjoy himself or so he said, and was off to the taverns."

"Any idea which tavern?"

"Yes, sir. In fact, the only one I know him to go to: The Sea Gull. It's right next to Sue Eller's Fancy House on the wharf, can't miss it."

"Thanks, Paul. I'll check there, then."

"No trouble, sir. I hope you find your wife and Mrs. Bonnet. She's a character, Mrs. Bonnet."

"Yes, she is."

It was very interesting to Daniel that the driver, Scotty, had disappeared also. In fact, it was rather eerie.

The waterfront in Bridgetown was a typical port, with pleasure houses, taverns, and run-down boarding houses.

He located The Sea Gull with no problems, thanks to Paul's good directions. He'd had no clue there were so many alehouses. He counted at least eight from here to the livery. Granted they all weren't on the waterfront, but that was quite a few for such a small town.

Stepping into the interior of the pub his nostrils flared. The smell was gruesome. He almost wished he'd not had breakfast. It was like bad fish, old sweat, and spilled rum.

The cliental was a scruffy lot. He looked for the men from Mrs. Delaney's description, but came up nil.

He'd not thought this was going to be easy, and it was proving an ordeal.

He pulled up a chair near the wall and rescanned the room. Mostly sailors and pirates from the looks of them. A few wenches waited tables; the poor things could use a good bath.

"Good morning, Governor. What can I be gettin' you?"

"Well, my dear lass. I'll have a pint of ale and if you like, I need some questions answered."

"Certainly then, I'll get your pint, and my name is Polly."

"Thank you, Polly."

What a nice gentleman in such a sleazy place. She wondered what kind of questions needed answers. She couldn't say much; last girl that did talk didn't come back from her bed. They said she died in her sleep but everyone knows someone did her in. Polly Thompson didn't plan on going out like that. No siree, she was going places. One day she'd meet a nice man like this one in the tavern. No more daydreaming, then.

"Here you are then and what questions did you 'ave?"

"Well first off, would you like to take a seat?"

"Surely," she said, easing her plump frame into the chair next to him and cozying up to his shoulder.

"Next, did you happen to see a carriage driver by the name of Scotty, yesterday?"

"Scotty? Oh yes, the cheeky fellow that drives Mrs. Bonnet's carriage?"

"Yes."

"He did come in for a pint or two, but then some other blokes started a fight with him."

"Did you see what happened?"

"Well they took him outside, didn't see him after that. Figured the fellow took himself home."

"What did the blokes in the fight look like?"

"You sure are inquisitive, ain't you?" she said rolling over in her mind if this information could get her throat slit.

Deciding that since the ones in question had left early on a ship headed out to sea, she decided to talk.

"Yes, their names was Rawlings and Slick, two nasty ones for sure. They work for a man named Lefty. Lefty Shakes, he used to be something of a pirate in his day, but after some sacking or other he twern't the same."

Daniel was filing these names in his mind. He wondered where Stede was this could turn out to be the news they needed.

"Do you know where they went?"

"Yes, sire, I do. The whole group left out this morning around five or so, back to sea."

Very convenient, thought Daniel. His best chance hauled up and took some precious cargo.

"Polly, you've been a wondrous help, but I've one quick question then I'll leave you alone."

"All right then."

"Do you happen to know which ship they left on?"

"Yes, that Cap'n Lefty fellow bought ole John Crow's ship. The name was the *Black Bird*. Hull's painted black with red letters. It's a morbid looking ship to be sure."

"Thank you so much, Polly," he said flipping her two gold sovereigns.

Polly caught the two shiny pieces and quickly stuffed then between her bosoms. That was plenty for her to get out this business now.

"Thank you, governor. If you ever need more help just let me know."

TWELVE

Daniel was pleased with all he'd learned from Polly. She'd been a great help. From her descriptions, he'd quickly left and found Stede.

"Lefty Shakes is the man in charge, Stede. Do you know anything about him?"

"Only that he's a *has-been* pirate. Which makes me wonder what sort of crazy scheme would make him take our girls. Personally I've never had dealings with him or the other two."

"Did you find anything out about your driver?"

"Unfortunately, yes. I was snooping around a bit and caught sight of my carriage parked out back of the alley behind one of the oceanfront taverns. It'd been covered in canvas and inside lay the body of Scotty. Evidently, he was in the way of those mad men." Stede rubbed his eyes with his hand.

Daniel could tell this had upset his friend dearly.

"Scotty was a good man and the things they'd done to his battered body were gruesome."

"Don't think of it Stede, we'll get this cleared up. I plan on setting sail this afternoon. I've already informed the crew and they were livid at the thought of someone taking Brianna."

"Any idea the direction they were headed?"

"I talked to one sailor who'd applied for work with this Cap'n Shakes, he'd been turned down for the job. Shakes had said he was to weak of character. He'd also said they were bound for Tortuga. Evidently, Shakes likes to talk, especially about his past prowess. The man said he kept bringing up a man named Hammock."

Daniel wouldn't swear by it, but for some reason that name pulled some invisible chord in his memory. Sometimes his amnesia was indeed a curse. He felt that by not remembering whose name that was he was missing a vital clue to this abduction.

"I've not heard of a man by the name of Hammock," Stede said. "That of course doesn't mean much. Have you enough supplies on board the *Enchantress* to make it to Tortuga?"

"Yes, I've done my best to order everything on quickly. We might be short on fresh bread until we get there, but we've survived on much less."

"Good then," Stede's expression was anything but peaceful. The man's eyes glowed with anger like he'd never seen from this kind man. It certainly boded ill for this ruthless cutthroat who'd stripped away their hearts.

"I can't sit idle by while you go on this rescue mission. The not knowing will drive me to despair."

"What will you do, Stede?" Daniel asked. He just hoped the man didn't do anything rash. They both needed to keep cool heads on this matter.

"I'm going to buy a ship and captain her myself. With both of us looking we'll have better luck running across the sea scum."

"Stede, are you sure? You've never sailed a ship before. Do you know enough to keep everything in order? I mean, I don't want to seem presumptuous, but sir, it's not as simple as a horse."

"I know that son and I appreicate your worries but this is something I have to do. My poor Patty is out there at the hands of these ruthless men and they will suffer dearly if they've harmed her in any way."

"I understand."

"I mean I won't rest until I see them punished!"

This said the two men stared morosely at the ocean. Each mulling their thoughts around like cheap wine. Headaches would definitely appear, but the two would try to weather this tempest out.

Stede was right, with two ships they were much more likely to run across this ship the *Black Bird*.

Turning to Stede, Daniel finally said, "I better be going if we're going to leave with the tide. Send me a message when you've chosen a ship and are ready to leave. It'll be hard, but I know we can do this."

Deep down he did have a feeling, blood boiling in controlled rage, he only waited to unleash the torrent that would explode when he meet up with Lefty Shakes, he'd pay dearly for this.

After Daniel left him standing at the rail, Stede's mind made some important decisions.

His purposeful stride was seen as he moved down the

wharf looking at the many anchored ships. His eyes took in the masts and hulls, not really seeing them still as they were now, but crashing through the waves on the way to save his Patty.

He was determined to find his contrary wife. At least this time her trouble was no fault of her own. She'd been in many scrapes over the years, usually social blunders and such, never something this serious.

His footsteps stopped in front of a nicely built smaller ship. It looked sleek and fast to Stede, which was exactly what he was looking for.

The name on the side said *The Swimming Porpoise*. That would have to be changed. It didn't suit him to be searching for pirates on a pleasantly titled ship. He needed something to get his point across. *Revenge* sounded nice to his ears. In the time it took to outfit the ship for leaving, the name could be baking on in the sun.

All that remained for him to do now was purchase this vessel from its current captain and find a crew. He'd even pay the sailors for their trouble. That would prevent a mutiny. His knowledge of seafaring ways was limited, but most men would work well for a decent wage.

The harbor was crawling with likely candidates and soon he'd rounded up close to seventy men. The ship had been purchased to the joy of the now richly endowed captain of the former *Swimming Porpoise*. He could live easy on the price he'd got from this crazy old man.

It annoyed Stede that he couldn't refit the ship more quickly. He was losing precious time lulling about in Bridgetown. His only hope was that Daniel was closing in on the ship called the *Black Bird*.

The quarters that Brianna and Patty were given were compact; more so than on the cruise ship that Brianna had left in 2007. At least the *Enchantment* had been clean. This hovel was filled with rats and wet leftover human refuse. Whoever had lived in the cell before hadn't fared well. The bones of a decomposed body lay chained at one end.

They had a small amount of light that filtered from a grate overhead, which gave them small amounts of hope.

The food was scarce, usually some sort of gruel and hard bread. They ate carefully, knowing the bread was full of black squirming weevils.

They were ignored mostly, except for these small meals. Evidently, the captain had ordered them private and to be kept unharmed until they reached the next port.

Neither knew where they were headed, nor what would become of them once they got to wherever it might be.

Occasionally they'd hear the crew talking. Mostly it was sailor-talk about female conquests, treasures, and their stories of battle. Every now and then they'd hear bits of information about the slimy captain himself.

Shortly after the incident with Daniel's father, it was unknown whether Captain Lefty Shakes would live or die. The damage that Mr. John Hammock's blade had done to the lower half of Shake's body had been often the butt of many crude sailors jokes. They'd hear, "Hey Franko, watch your step in that rigging or you'll end up to *Shake-n* to meet your lady love," or "Watch ole Pete over there, he'll *Shake* the life right out of ya!"

The guffaws and sniggers stopped when the object of their humor appeared on deck.

Often Shakes would say, "What are all you scalawags laughing about?"

Some sort of explanation would be given, but not the truth. Although the crew made light of the captain's disability, they did fear his wrath. He was known as being a terror, especially when in one of his psycho rages. He'd as soon kill a mate as look at him.

One thing Brianna had noted about this day and age was that people respected crazy. When someone whose lights weren't all on was in charge, there was fear and respect. She figured they must go hand in hand. Pirates were a filthy lot. Control was important. Mutiny was a fear all in charge had. One had to rule with a heavy fist to remain on top of everything.

Patty was doing her best to control her rising terror. Both girls had overheard Rawlings and Slick talking, the fate of that dear lady was grim.

Shakes idea of a ransom hadn't sat well with the mangy duo. They both liked the idea of keeping the beautiful women. Patty had expressed to Brianna her fear of rape. Ever since the closet episode of her youth the thought of rape sent her into a frozen terror, like a bird caught in the eye of a snake. She just didn't know what she'd do in that situation.

"I just don't know what I'd do," remarked the pale faced Patty. "The thought of those brutes touching me is so frightening."

"I know Patty, hopefully it'll never happen. But if so it's best to be prepared."

"I'm so glad we're in this ordeal together. I just don't know how I'd have survived without your kind reassurances."

"Oh, Patty, you'd have done fine, but the bad thing is you're in this mess because of me."

"Don't say that, dear!"

"Well, its true. This stupid captain only grabbed us up to get at Daniel. If it'd been me snatched alone, you'd have been safe."

"Don't dwell on the *ifs* or *should'ves*. We both got to stay positive like you said, there's no sense in letting the fear over take us."

"You're right, Patty. I'm sorry for being so melodramatic."

"It's alright, dear, I'm … what is it you said before? Quite the *drama queen* myself."

It was nice having Patty here. She guessed if Patty would have been in the future she'd been diagnosed as bipolar or something. Not that she stayed down and out long, but her mood swings were amazing.

The ships speed slowed down. They could feel the sails being altered in direction.

"Land ho!" one sailor cried from above.

"Looks like we'll be docking soon," Brianna remarked.

Rawlings' grinning face was soon seen at the door.

"You ladies is in for a fine treat. We've brought you to the wonderful island of Tortuga. Be prepared to go ashore."

"Tortuga," said Brianna. "I never thought I'd see the stronghold of pirates. It is kind of exciting."

"I, for one, am not that excited," stated Patty.

"It's the history that intrigues me so. I know my life's backwards now, but it thrills me to be alive in the land of brotherhood."

"I'm glad you're pleased, dear," a non-smiling Patty said.

"Oh, don't get in the slumps now Patty. Soon we'll be on wonderful land again."

Knowing what Brianna said about being on land again did lift the flagging spirits of Patricia Bonnet. Land would indeed be refreshing. She'd had enough of sea travel for quite a while.

Rawlings and his shadow, Slick, arrived about an hour later.

"Alright, then. You two get to go back into these sacks. We can't have the locals seeing such pretty faces. They might have it in mind then to steal ole Shake's purities. Can't have that now, can we?"

"That's right, ladies, in you go."

Knowing that to protest would be futile, leading to bruises or worse, they quickly complied.

The smell of the potato sacks was much more pleasant than the smell of this chamber and their grungy escorts.

Flopped across the shoulders of the men and carried down a long plank, following their fanatic leader, the five made good progress through the sparse crowd.

Today was an off day in the harbor. Many pirates had left on one trail or another. All loved treasure and any hint at a ship or group of ships caused a commotion as the eager exploration hunters pursued the dreams of riches.

Lefty Shakes and his lovely cargo arrived at the stately home of an old colleague soon after starting their trip.

Lefty had known Blue Eyed Charlie for years. They'd started their careers together under the same captain some forty-five years back.

Knocking on the door Lefty couldn't help warning the women.

"Blue Eyed Charlie is not a man to be crossed ladies. If I were you, I'd not speak unless spoken to. I've seen him carve the tongue out of many a woman who crossed his ways."

About that time the door opened and a woman of an ancient age opened the door.

"What would you be wanting, sir?"

"Why, you old crone, it's me, Cap'n Lefty Shakes and I'm here to visit with Blue Eyed Charlie, himself. He knows me well and would be highly annoyed to know you were rude to such a good friend."

"Fine then," said the crone. "I'll go fetch Charlie myself. You can drop your charges in the room across the hall and wait in the room across from it. There's spirits in the sideboard, so help yourselves."

"She's an old bat ain't she, Cap'n?

"Yes, but that old bat's been through more pirate days than you slobs have seen. She's cutthroat through and through. They called her Slapjack Molly in her hay day."

"Why's that?" inquired Slick.

"Her tongue was sharper than the snap of the Union Jack in the wind. Not to mention, she had a terrible penchant for slapping the teeth right out of your mouth if were close enough to cross her," Lefty smiled a leering smile of remembrance. "In fact, before she'd gotten so used up I'd been slapped by her a couple times myself."

Rawlings couldn't imagine bedding down with something that horrible. He had to admit that the crone was old.

Maybe she'd looked better in her younger days. Besides, considering it was Lefty Shakes, beggars couldn't be choosy.

The men dropped the two hog-tied women in the designated room. Noticing the bars on the windows and the thick padlock locking them inside, those two would be stowed away safely.

The sacks were removed and ropes cut again. If this worked out to Lefty's liking, he could turn a quick profit in the slave market with the both of them, once he'd killed Daniel Storme.

Molly had announced the arrival of Lefty Shakes and his men to the renowned Blue Eyed Charlie.

Charlie could only wonder at what had brought the joyful slug to his doorstep. It seemed to him that every time Lefty arrived he brought trouble.

The startling blue eyes that had given him his nickname squinted in bothered agitation. His current job in the traffic of human cargo was going well and he had no need of a toad like Shakes messing up his well-planned operation.

"What brings you to visit, Lefty? I thought you'd given up wandering the sea for a quiet tavern life."

"Well, I had all but decided life was a bore, until I discovered some unfinished business from years ago."

"Really, what business would that be?"

"Do you remember John Hammock?"

"Yes, how could I forget the man who gave you that awful scar? What of him? I thought you'd killed that one year's ago?"

"I did. That quitting snake didn't have a chance, but his son had gotten away."

Lefty's claw-like fingers stroked his chin in thoughtful consideration. "Until now I'd long thought the whelp had drowned, but come to find out he's alive and well and bought a place near Bridgetown."

"I'm guessing you'll get your revenge then," said Blue Eyed Charlie, wondering when he'd know the real reason for Lefty's visit. "That's all fine and good but where do I come in?"

"I've brought you some fine woman flesh. Thought between the two of us we'd make a pretty coin or two. One just happens to be the whelp's wife."

Aw, so that's the catch, thought Charlie.

"Where would those ladies be?"

"We locked them in the room across the way, Molly said that was best."

"Yes, she's right. Well, let's go see if they're worth the trouble."

Brianna felt nasty. She hoped she'd not picked up any jumping hitchhikers in her hair. She wouldn't be surprised as dirty as the ship had been.

At least in the house, the room was clean. Patty had used the washstand near one of the windows just to get some of the grime off. Brianna had quickly followed suit.

The thought of being clean again would be great if it were possible. Their biggest worry was what would happen to them now.

The lock grating in the door told them they had guests.

"These here are our girls. A little scruffy right now, but they'll clean up real nice," said Rawlings.

Blue Eyed Charlie surveyed the two with a critical eye. The blonde would bring a nice fortune from the Turks. That golden hair, although needing a good washing, still had a healthy sheen. Her eyes were stunning, too. Next was the brunette. This one wasn't in her prime, but was still a beauty. Some rich man looking for a mature doll to add to his collection might go for that one.

"Not bad," Charlie said to Lefty. "Let's get them cleaned up and fed properly and then we'll talk."

Lefty knew that was a good sign. If Charlie hadn't been interested he could have always sold them cheaper to a local fancy house, but with the approval of the renowned white slave dealer, he would make a nice profit indeed.

Rawlings and Slick would be disappointed to lose the one called Patricia, but they were almost to the limit of their usefulness and would have to be eliminated anyways.

The door closed and they waited, both lost in thought as to the conversation they'd heard. Exactly who was Blue Eyed Charlie, and why were they here?

That mean spirited Shake's man had looked pleased with himself. That could only bode ill for the two.

A knock and the sound of the key opening made them both look up to see the one called Molly come in bearing a food covered tray.

"Eat up, lovies. After your dinner I'll send in some buckets and a tub and we'll scrub that nasty filth off ye."

"Thank you," Brianna said.

"Don't think on it, love. Best rest up. You've gotta get yourselves rested and groomed."

"What for might I ask?" Patty questioned.

"Now don't you be worrying none about that, dearie. You'll find out soon enough."

With that said she exited, locking the door on the way out. She'd learned long ago that the pretty women Blue Eyed Charlie chose for his clients could be sneaky. He didn't take to well to the pretty things escaping. She'd learned that long ago and had lost two fingers in repayment for the man's loss. She didn't have the urge to lose anymore. At her age, it might just kill her.

THIRTEEN

Enchantress and her crew were making good time. Daniel figured Stede wouldn't be too far behind. The man's determination had been too strong for him not to be.

Spirits had been high on the trip. Everyone aboard couldn't wait to have a chance to help the Captain and his lady. All who had met Brianna on board had been charmed by her kindness.

Tommy was ready to join the fight. Daniel had already told the lad that he could help better by staying safe. He'd told him that he'd need to be on board, making sure the cabin was ready. He looked Tommy in the eye, man to man, and said, "We don't know if Brianna might be hurt physically or injured emotionally. She'll need care and good people near her to reassure her."

Tommy had been mollified. If it were his important job to keep Mrs. Brianna feeling secure, then he'd do his best.

Wally was also upset. He cursed his age, time and again. If this would have happened when he was a wee bit spryer he'd have tore the rascal from limb to limb.

"How're you holding up, Daniel?" asked a pensive Peter Swallows.

"I'm doing my best. I keep going over the names in my mind and still can't recall where I've heard the name Hammock."

"Don't think on it too much. You could have only heard it in passing."

"True enough," Daniel still felt deep down that it was more than a name heard from some obscure place.

The answer he sought would have to wait until their arrival in Tortuga. For now, he could ponder all he liked, but until then, his conclusions would only be guesses.

Peter hated to see his friend under such stress. He'd only known a couple weeks of his wife's love before it'd been ripped away. There always were madmen wandering around the world leaving havoc in their wake.

The pistols had been primed and the knives all sharpened in readiness for a fight. Tortuga wasn't known for being peaceful.

Daniel had dealt with his share of dreaded pirates over the years. The Smithfield's shipping line had lost little cargo to the devilish leeches. It wasn't luck, it was just known that the Smithfield line was well armed and most of the crew had in one way or another, learned to fight. Often fights of life or death.

The captain was certain that they'd find Brianna. He couldn't help dwelling on what was happening to her. The scars of fear and blood could be life long.

He'd focus his moments on more positive things. There was still much to do before they reached the island of the pirate brotherhood. From his calculations, only half a day behind the *Black Bird*, he was betting that the crusty Cap'n Lefty wouldn't be expecting him this soon.

"Brianna, isn't it glorious to be clean again?"

"Indeed it is Patty, amazing how washing away all that dirt and sweat makes you feel almost human. If it weren't for being locked up in this room, like the prize turkey at Thanksgiving, I'd really be in better spirits."

Now that Patty knew her past, Brianna didn't feel obligated to talk so proper. She understood that half the time Patty didn't know what she was referring to, but she seemed to get the gist.

"You have such colorful analogies, almost makes me wish I knew more of the future."

"Don't trouble yourself over much. The simplicity of now is much better."

"You call being held prisoner by pirates *simple?*"

"Well, not really, but it's a whole lot more exciting than office work. Just picture it, Patty, all day surrounded by books, ledgers, numbers, and notes. That's enough to drive you mad."

The freedom from the abyss of cubical Hades was not bad at all.

The windows in their room had afforded them a great view of the harbor. Located on a small knoll this home had breathtaking views. Even considering this was currently their prison, convicts at Folsom never had a view like this and Brianna wasn't one to sing the blues for long. Her optimism always pushed its way forward.

Molly arrived bearing her usual tray of delights. The chef wasn't the most fancy, but could make some wonderful fresh bread. Smear some butter on that and it was quite tasty.

"My you two certainly have improved over yesterday.

Quite the mongrels you two were, wouldn't know you now if'n I hadn't seen it with my own two eyes."

Molly would be sure to report the news to Blue Eyed Charlie. He was at this moment sending out reports of his latest acquisitions to his best clients. One was a sheik from Arabia and the other was a prince in Turkey. Both loved and collected beautiful women like porcelain dolls. It mattered not to the profit-seeking slave trader if the man treated them well or not. His worry lay in the turn of the coin.

After one night in his home, the women were already on the mend. Their room although barred was spacious and neat. Comfortable beds were on each side of the double windows. A washstand and set of clean chamber pots, which the ever-present Molly had cleaned that morning, completed the room.

Lefty Shakes had discovered how the talents of his lowly cohorts had reached its limit. The two had noisily complained in front of the trader about the loss and lack of pleasure they'd enjoyed from the captives. They'd also challenged their pay and asked for more.

Overall the two tried his patience to the breaking point. Tonight he'd have Molly fix them some of her special spice pudding. The spice being an ample dose of hemlock, which would eliminate a growing sore spot in his life.

Rawlings was simply too cocky for his own good and Slick was such a dumb lamb, he probably would fall off a cliff if Rawlings went first.

Knowing it would be only a matter of time before the

whelp showed up, he knew he'd have to warn Charlie and set up some sort of defensive strategy.

It was lucky for Lefty that Charlie had seen such promise in the wife of the brat. He could almost see the greed wheels turning in the traders mind last night at dinner. He'd go on and on about how rare it was to find a blonde that had green eyes and was beautiful. The other wasn't quite as good, but he still felt the women would sell at a better price than he usually made.

Lefty planned to explain the husband problem to Charlie tonight at dinner, with the man's greed glowing in his eyes, he knew he'd not have any trouble getting the protection he required.

Such sweet revenge. He'd kill the son of that old enemy and sell his wife into slavery. A sweeter concoction would be hard to find.

Blue Eyed Charlie grinned in self-satisfied delight. Luck was with him indeed for a Turkish slave trader had pulled into harbor two days ago. One of his long time partners in deal-ings was even staying at his home on the island. He'd sent a message telling the man of his good fortune of finding two lovely creatures and had received a reply back saying he'd be most pleased to see his latest selections. Ackmed Mohamed was now on his way here for dinner.

He'd sent Molly to ready the women.

It was said of Blue Eyed Charlie that his slaves were the cleanest and least abused of the Caribbean market. Charlie believed in quality products. Abuse showed up too readily and made prices lower. It was to his benefit that the other traders didn't understand the philosophy.

His cliental would always surpass those of the lesser ilk. He was a gentleman slaver after all. His reputation for beauty was renowned.

Now all he had to do was get rid of Cap'n Lefty Shakes for a while. The man carried creepiness about him that he didn't want affecting this sale.

"Speak of the devil," spoke Charlie as Lefty Shakes strolled into the room. "Good, Lefty, just the man I wanted to see. I've a rich merchant coming to dinner tonight to look into our mutual interest."

"Excellent, I'll be glad to meet him."

"Well Lefty, you see. This man is Turkish. The Turks are easily offended. I thought if you were agreeable, I'd handle the interview. Besides, I've known this man for years and we have a certain relationship."

Lefty knew this was a fancily worded way at getting his crude self out of sight and didn't really care. If Blue Eyed Charlie thought he'd be careless and cause the deal to go sour he was wrong.

"Sounds fine, at my age it's nice to plot my schemes and rest. You meet this Turk and get the deal settled."

He'd not thought the man had it in him to bow out gracefully, but he'd done a fine job of it. He must want something.

"There is one more thing, Charlie."

"What would that be?"

"The blonde has a husband, who'll be on the way here. He's not pleased that I took her. If you want to keep your investment we'll have to defend both. The other's husband is

Stede Bonnet. He's some plantation owner on Barbados, not much of a threat, but the other I'd like to punish."

"Fine then, I'll tell Rodrigo to post extra guards and whatever else he feels might be necessary."

"Wonderful, well I'll get out of your way so you can prepare for your meeting."

"Rest well, then."

"And enjoy your interview."

Daniel's luck had finally run out. The good wind that had been blowing upon leaving Barbados had ceased. They were located somewhere near the south of Jamaica and had lost the strong flow.

This was not a time to be becalmed. Time was essential. Brianna needed him and he was not going to break his promise to protect her.

All aboard were worried for the captain's sake. He'd lost weight and had a frightening look in his eyes.

"I've never seen the lad so distraught," remarked Wally to Peter.

"It's definitely a change from his usually jovial self." Peter's own fear for the safety of Brianna and Mrs. Bonnet was even worse than that which plagued Captain Storme. Peter knew the fate that could be in store for the ladies.

Peter had been sold into slavery at the age of eight. He recalled that he'd never enjoyed his youth as the cabin boy Tommy was allowed. He'd been forced to clean the feet of a smuggler named Martin Webster.

Webster was known for having a penchant for young boys.

Needless to say young Peter's days were spent entertaining his obese, hairy owner. Each task assigned to the boy had been distasteful and humiliating. Webster knew to keep the boy well flogged and busy. Idle hands were the devil's workplace. He'd heard Webster repeat that line over and over.

Ironically, the work he forced the boy to do was indeed the work of the devil. Often Peter was kept in chains having not had a spirit that wasn't easily controlled. The scars on his back paid tribute to that fact. The burn of the cat still haunted his eyes. He'd escaped as soon as he was strong enough to overpower his fat proprietor.

His age was fourteen and he'd exercised daily to build his muscles. Where the sloth like Webster had previously overpowered Peter by sheer weight, Peter could now defend himself from the man's amorous advances by strength.

He'd knocked the man senseless and made a run for the coast. Martin Webster was a sad excuse for a smuggler. He'd only smuggle when he needed money to supply his opium habit. It'd been to his benefit to have the handsome boy as a slave. Once his skull had been brained during his charges escape, he'd promptly used up the last of his opium and been shot trying to steal a goose, which he swore had mocked him, and told him to eat it.

Peter's escape ended him hiding out in a small fishing village. A ship had docked looking for able hands and he'd signed on. His life had steadily improved from that time on, but the years of enslavement at the hands of that boar-like man instilled in him a deep hate of the slave trade.

It wasn't meant for people to own others. He knew Tortuga was alive and full of the offending trade and with beauties like Brianna and Mrs. Bonnet, a man involved in stealing such would lean highly in favor of making a sell. He just hoped he was wrong.

"Once we get Brianna back, I predict our captain will be right as rain."

Peter wondered if Wally's optimistic statement would indeed prove true.

"I hope you're proved correct, Wally, for all our sakes. I worry that if something bad happened to them that Daniel would take it out on himself. The worry alone is affecting his health."

The object of their conversation could be seen pacing the deck.

"Just a good gust or two, please, Lord, help me get to Tortuga. I've a promise to keep. I can't let her down. Please, Lord," his mind worked over and over across plans, obstacles, and more. It'd been four hours since the last good breeze. Surely this wait would end soon.

Molly had worked for Blue Eyed Charlie for twenty years or more. The work hadn't been bad. She was to take care of the pretty girls and every now and then dispose of some unwanted nuisance. She prided herself on good work. Today was like every other. She'd been told to dress up the women in proper attire and ready them for an inspection. At dinner a prospective buyer would review them, and Molly herself, would possibly end up with a bonus depending on how good of terms were offered.

She sighed as she carried the folded garments to the chamber allotted to the two. Opening the door she said, "Afternoon, lovies, I've brought you a pair of lovely gowns to wear, the fit should be good. I've an eye for such things." She'd picked out two guaranteed to set off the features of the wearers.

Brianna and Patty were pleased to change out of their old gowns. Neither had been washed and were frayed and picking up a terrible odor. The long ride on the nasty ship certainly didn't help any. The soft fabrics and warm colors of the new clothes made them a glory to don.

"I'll take care of these filthy things while you pretties enjoy being completely clean," she said scooping up the offending articles. "I'll be by later to take you on a stroll. There'll be a gentleman here who wants to meet you both," with a quick check around the room to assure herself that things were in order and nothing amiss she then left the room closing the door firmly behind her.

"Our Molly's quite a busy bee."

"She certainly is," Brianna said. "I wonder who the mystery man is."

"From all the information we've been given, I don't have any idea."

"My wonder, dear Patty, is what kind of business does Mr. Blue Eyed Charlie deal in. He doesn't appear to be a normal pirate and if not that, then what is he?"

"I'm just glad we have something different to wear."

"Me too, I was starting to wonder if we'd be wearing those until they rotted."

Patty was quick to notice how flattering the gowns were. She remembered from her long study of clothing throughout the years that there was always a reason for looking your best. Who could the gentleman, as Molly called him, be? Why would they be asked to meet him? It all was very peculiar to her.

"Brianna, you'd don't supposed that this Blue Eyed Charlie fellow could be a slave trader, do you?"

Piecing together the bits and pieces they'd overheard and what she knew of Tortuga Island, the possibility was very real.

"I suppose it's possible, Patty—" at her friend's ashen look she rushed on, "—but surely we'd have known that by now. Maybe the man's just here to talk about a ransom or something."

Brianna knew her words sounded less than sure. She had a feeling deep down that Patty's conclusion would prove right.

"Patty, don't worry, we'll know everything soon enough. Why don't we play some cards, again?"

Brianna had talked Molly into giving them a deck to while away the long hours of solitude. Molly, seeing no harm in the idea, had quickly complied.

"I'm sure your right. Don't borrow trouble and all."

"What shall we play?"

"How about that poker game you taught me?"

"Sounds fine."

They played for what seemed like ages, but at a quick glance to Brianna's watch she noted it'd only been thirty-five minutes. Oh, what a long afternoon. Where was Daniel anyways? Surely he'd be here soon. She knew he'd be on her trail.

FOURTEEN

Mr. Stede Bonnet's long wait to depart Bridgetown had finally ended. He'd wandered the town searching for hints and clues throughout the area. He'd come to the conclusion that Cap'n Lefty Shakes had used the Sea Gull Tavern as his main place of operation. His questions had all assured him that old Lefty was all but dried up. He'd also talked to a woman who cleaned the backrooms of the tavern. She'd found some fabric that'd been left in a room Lefty was known to use. It'd been a small strip of Patty's lace. He'd know the pattern anywhere and was sure that's why she'd placed it there.

His dear wife would know he'd not rest until she was found.

The *Revenge* was ready to leave port. He'd only now moved his things aboard. The crew had already seen to putting things in order. All they awaited was his signal.

During his wait, he'd studied up on nautical terms and such. He hoped to impress his paid for crew. Respect could be easily lost if he wasn't careful. He'd tried to choose men from the grogshops, which had some sort of semblance of honor. At least he'd tried his best.

"Weigh anchor and set sail men! We've quite a lot of distance to cover and I'd like to make good time!"

"Yes, Captain!" echoed across the ship.

Slowly, *Revenge* eased her way into the beautiful currents of the Caribbean Sea.

Ackmed Mohamed stepped off the carriage that'd brought him to the home of his longtime associate Blue Eyed Charlie. So far Ackmed's trip had been uneventful and he'd been pleased to receive the message from the trader.

The markets in the east were starving for exotic beauties. He'd promised several of his clients that he'd keep his eyes open for fresh faces. It always made him marvel at the obsession for beauty that some men had. They were never happy with the various exotics they possessed and always wanted more.

Not that he was complaining. His chosen profession kept his coffers full. He was himself a man of rich taste and his profits over the years helped him keep his expensive lifestyle.

The ever-present Molly greeted him at the door.

"Come in, Mr. Mohamed, Mr. Charlie is in the study. I'll announce you, if you'll follow this way."

"Thank you, Molly."

"Don't mention it, sir."

Knocking on the study door, Molly called, "Mr. Mohamed's here, sir."

"Ackmed, glad you could come."

"It is I who will hopefully be glad, my friend."

"Yes, I think you'll be quite pleased," Charlie said, stacking some papers and putting them aside. He prized himself on his bookwork, not many traders or pirates kept records, but Blue Eyed Charlie knew it was the best way to see how his investments were working out. He'd been keeping notes and invoices on his dealings for years and he could see the positive build up of his gold in organized black and white.

"Shall we enjoy dinner or would you prefer a drink?"

"Let us enjoy our meal and then I'd like to view your prospects."

"Excellent then, Molly?" he called.

"Yes, sir," she said peeping around the doorway corner.

"Tell cook that we'll dine first."

"Yes, sir."

Both men rose and trailed into the ornately decorated dining room. Delicate gilt covered the mirrors on the walls and the table was laid out with the finest bone china and crystal that could be found in a lair full of pirates.

"As always, your table is a treat to behold."

"Thank you, Ackmed. You know it's not every day I can entertain someone with your selective tastes. It warms me to know you approve."

The dinner consisted of a meal fit for a king. Ackmed was again astounded at his friend's good manners. Charlie had done well to build such wealth from nothing and to start out in ignorance on the sea. This man had definitely made a name for himself. It was one of the things he liked about him. His vanity often helped him get a better deal where he'd have otherwise paid too much for the slaves.

"I made a great profit off the last slaves we agreed upon,

particularly the red-headed one with the curls. She alone sold for more than half I got for the others."

"I'm glad you were able to do well. I've only two for you to appraise currently, quality has been hard to come by lately."

"I agree. I've been delaying my trip home in hopes of discovering another profit such as I had last."

"I believe you'll have to look no further after today."

"Well, my friend, you have certainly gained my interest. Let us see what you have acquired."

Molly was sent to fetch the women. On the way there, Lefty Shakes halted her in the hallway.

"Molly, dear, I need a favor of you."

"Fine, Lefty, but you'll have to wait until after Mr. Mohamed leaves."

"Oh, it won't take but a minute of your time."

"Out with it then."

If Molly was anyone other than who she was, he'd be liable to backhand her, but he knew better than to offend one as knowing as she.

"You know the two men who arrived with me?"

"Yes, what of 'em?"

"Would it be possible for you to dispose of them? They've become a thorn in my side."

"I'll see what can be done," she said, trying not to be obvious in her dislike. "Now if you don't mind, I'm to fetch the ladies."

"Alright then, thank you, Molly."

Molly had no intention of helping the old fool. He could

do his own dirty work. He didn't pay her wages and she'd not built up any fondness of him either.

Rawlings and Slick had made camp near the kitchen and they'd been sleeping in the loft of the barn and visiting the kitchen daily. They both agreed that Blue Eyed Charlie was a man of good food and alcohol. Everything was kept well stocked and they were left to their own devices.

Things had been going too well

"Rawlings. I've got a bit of a bad news to tell you," said Slick, walking into the kitchen.

"What might that be?" he asked, not really listening. Slick was always known for having bad news.

"I overheard Lefty talking to the maid named Molly. You remember the one. She t'was the one you called a crone," at Rawlings nod of agreement he continued. "He was asking her to get rid of us. What you suppose that means?"

"Sounds like Lefty's plotting trouble. What did the crone say?"

"Didn't say anything positive about it. In fact, when Lefty turned his back, she made quite a face. Don't think she's to fond of him neither."

"Well then, we'll just have to take what's ours and leave."

"Where will we go, Rawlings?"

"Don't you worry your head about it, I'll take care of everything."

"I knew you would," he said with honest admiration.

Brianna and Patty marched unceremoniously down the hallway and into the study. Both men had retired to this room to enjoy the comfort of Charlie's plush leather chairs.

Upon the entrance of the two ladies, Ackmed's interest was immediately launched in the direction of Brianna. His gaze took in her glowing hair and comely figure. When her eyes lifted to meet his in open curiosity he was startled at the color. They sparkled somewhere between green and gold. His eyes moved to Patty and his appraisal wasn't near as long.

"You've outdone yourself again, my friend," remarked Ackmed. "Both are very lovely. May I examine closer?"

"Be my guest, Ackmed. You know I always want you completely satisfied with your purchase."

This caused the fear to race in Brianna's veins. She dared not glance at Patty. She could already feel the tension burning from her direction. So Blue Eyed Charlie was a slave trader. Again, Brianna was fascinated with the situation she was in.

Ackmed arose and traveled the distance from his chair to the women in two short strides. He walked in front of both, looking at their eyes, ears, and even being presumptuous enough to open their mouths to look at their teeth!

Knowing how perilous her predicament, was Brianna endured in silence. She could act out, but knew it was better to pretend docility. Ackmed noticed the fear in the older of the two. He admitted the brunette was a lovely lady. Her age could be a problem, but the beauty was there. The younger lady carried herself well. He could tell she was repressing many thoughts. Here was one with spirit, she could pretend her acceptance, but he knew better. She was a fighter and glorious to look at too.

"I feel it only right to consider their purchase carefully. I'll take tonight to come to a decision as to my offers. Tomorrow I'll be back to finalize our transaction."

"Sounds fine, Ackmed. Take all the time you like and I'll await your decision on the morrow."

After this comment Molly again herded them to the room they considered their cell.

"That went well, lovies. I've not seen Mr. Mohamed so pleased in quite a while."

"I'm glad he's happy," sulked Brianna. She knew he'd seen through her guise and it didn't sit well. She thought she could hide her emotions better than that.

"Ah, now, don't be carrying on so. You'll both be pleased as parrots in no time. Rich men will take care of you the rest of your lives. Not bad if you ask me."

Brianna chose not to comment. She was more worried about Patty. The dear lady appeared to be in a state of fearful shock.

"Patty, are you all right?"

There was no answer and Brianna feared the worst. Now was not the time for one of Patty's fits of depression. She helped her to lie down and rested a pillow underneath her head.

"Brianna?"

"Yes, Patty. What is it?"

"I had a awful premonition when we walked into that room," she rubbed her forehead and continued. "Something bad is going to happen."

"Patty, I know things look bad, but we'll survive. We have so far."

"I know dear, but I've got a feeling that prickles my skin and that usually bodes ill."

"Listen, you're probably just tired. It's been hard on both

of us the past week. Why don't you lie down and rest and we'll talk more in the morning."

"I'll try to rest. You're right, this week has been terribly tiring."

After Brianna heard Patty's breathing slow she tried to stop her own worries. Slaves. She was to be a slave. If only Daniel would hurry. What if he never came? Oh, she knew he would, though. He'd lost too much. She knew he'd best the crook Lefty Shakes. That was a longstanding debt Lefty would have to pay. She could only imagine Daniel's anger at that man when he knew the whole truth.

Rawlings and Slick waited until late that night to accomplish their plan. It was close to midnight and the door to the women's quarters was easy to find. The moon was full and casting a bright light through a window at the far end of the hall.

It took Slick only a moment to pick the large old lock. The door opened with only a few squeaks. Inside they could make out the two women sleeping peacefully. Thankfully the windows offered enough light to distinguish the two.

Rawlings crept over to the woman who'd plagued his mind since the kidnapping in Barbados. Their plan was simple. They'd take the one named Patricia and leave the other for the profit of Blue Eyed Charlie. They had no quarrel with him, but Lefty Shakes owed them.

Slick quietly removed some rope and they quickly bound the sleeping woman up. The ladies were sleeping soundly thanks to the potion Molly had put in their tea. She'd not meant to help these thieves, but it was working out well for the scoundrels.

They lifted the small woman into their arms, moved towards the door, and refastened the lock. The discovery wouldn't be made until morning and by then they'd be long gone.

Rawlings had been sure to get on friendly terms with Charlie's guards. When the pair emerged carrying the rolled bundle, the guards only waved and let them pass.

After the conversation with Slick, Rawlings had made his way to the outer part of town. There he'd located a deserted shack, which would work out nicely for what he had planned.

Now as they moved silently through the streets and reached the outskirts of the town, he recalled the provisions he'd had Slick retrieve.

"Did you get everything, Slick?"

"Yes, I double checked it all. We should be set up well for a couple weeks."

"Good job. It'll definitely be a respite from the company of the scurvy Lefty Shakes. He'll not double-cross the likes of me."

Slick nodded in agreement. Rawlings was one man who scared him thoughtless. That's one reason they were friends. Slick knew he didn't have the cunning to survive without the protection Rawlings offered.

Molly arrived early the next morning. She wanted to check on the ladies and make sure they had rested well. She noticed something fishy as soon as she saw the door. The lock had a handful of scratches across the faceplate. It looked as if someone had broken in.

Opening the door with her key, she saw Brianna sleeping soundly, but on the other bed Patty was missing. A stealthy search of the room confirmed it. Someone had broken in and taken Patty.

She'd go tell Blue Eyed Charlie and he'd figure out who'd done this.

Charlie was having a breakfast of kidney and eggs, when the appearance of Molly looking upset caused him to quit chewing.

"What is it Molly? You look a fright."

"It's the one named Patricia, sir, someone's took her."

"Took her? Who'd do that?"

"I'm thinking you might be asking Cap'n Lefty Shakes. He asked me to kill his two cohorts. I wonder if they did this to get at him."

"I'll ask him directly," he said. "Was the blonde still there?"

"Yes sir, untouched and still restin' from her tea."

"Good, she's the largest profit in the venture. As long as we still have her, we'll do just fine, but Lefty has a lot to answer for."

Brianna slept the morning away. The tea had been strong. She hoped that Patty had slept well.

She tried to get up quietly in case Patty was still sleeping across the room. She did her usual morning things and glanced across the room.

Patty was gone!

She wondered if Molly might have taken her somewhere, but seeing the shoes on the floor by the bed she guessed not.

Molly arrived around noon with her usual meal.

"Molly, where's Patty?"

"We had a little mishap this morning but don't think on it. It'll be took care of."

"But Molly, what happened?"

"Well, lovey, evidently the two slobs that arrived with you—"

"Rawlings and Slick?"

"Yes, those are the ones. They snuck in here and took the sleeping Patty. We don't know where yet, but Charlie's looking into it."

Brianna remembered Patty's fearful premonition. She only hoped the crooks would be caught soon.

"Why did we sleep so deeply?"

"Oh, I put something to sooth your nerves in the tea. Makes one sleep well, almost like the dead."

Personally that was a little spooky. A sleep so sound you'd not know you'd been taken from your bed seemed wrong. She'd be more careful with Molly's trays from now on.

Her fear for Patty increased as the day passed. Soon she knew the man named Ackmed Mohamed would arrive to talk to Blue Eyed Charlie about prices for the two slaves. She wondered if he'd explain the missing Patty or just offer her alone.

Blue Eyed Charlie had no intention of telling Ackmed about the disappearance of Patricia Bonnet. His idea was to tell him that the lady had taken ill and they'd discuss everything once she was well again.

Ackmed arrived at a quarter after five. His thoughts had spun on what he could get for the green-eyed doll. Such features would fetch him a good price indeed. He'd be careful to not let Charlie know how truly interested he was.

Molly announced him and he was once more in the presence of the distinguished trader.

"Good to see you again, Ackmed."

"And you my friend."

"I hope your sleep was restful."

"Yes, I slept well, but enough pleasantries. I'd like to settle our business quickly. I've a few more stops to make before I retire for the evening and it looks as though a storm is brewing off the coast."

"I understand. These Caribbean storms can be unpredictable."

The discussion ensued. Each politely rolling numbers through the room until an agreement was made. Once the deal was struck the men shook hands and Ackmed Mohamed started on his way.

The boom of thunder could be heard to the southeast. Black dark clouds were easing their way across the horizon darkening the afternoon to almost night.

His first thought was to hurry home to the safety therein, but he knew he had to visit some shops and a few more slave traders before retiring for the night. He hoped the woman with dark hair named Patricia felt better soon. His ship needed to leave soon. If she didn't that was fine, at least he'd still have the prize.

Even her name flowed around her. Brianna, like a river moving downstream, the syllables suited her regality.

Blue Eyed Charlie was left in a quandary. Questioning Cap'n Lefty Shakes had been useless. The dolt had truly believed Molly would have taken care of his problems. It had been her choice. Although, if she had killed them this problem wouldn't have arisen.

He'd not blame her, though. Over the years her services had proved so useful. His lovely slaves had always been rested and clean. Molly certainly wasn't the issue now. Lefty Shakes would have to locate his backward men.

Of course he could always send Rodrigo to find something out. After being made into a fool by the man named Rawlings, he wasn't very fond of him and would readily send some assassins to retrieve the stolen woman.

Yes, he'd tell Rodrigo, before the troublesome sea dogs had too much time to ruin the lovely lady.

FIFTEEN

The stillness of the sea would be interrupted by evening. Dark silhouettes grew upon the horizon and with the dark clouds would be the wind Daniel so needed.

The storm would surely be strong from the looks of the sky. They'd weathered many out and would use this one to their advantage. The dullness and lack of motion would end and the journey to Tortuga could continue.

By afternoon, the rain started along with fierce gusts of wind. Each crewman moved in perfect response to all that nature was unleashing. The fury of the night to come wasn't anything compared to the fury raging within the soul of Captain Daniel Storme.

Daniel stood at the wheel with his legs apart, drenched in the heavy rain and sending challenging looks toward the sky. His prayers had been answered. Now it was up to him to see the ship safely to harbor where he could then confront the hated Cap'n Lefty Shakes.

By morning the power of the storm had blown itself out. The blue sky could be seen peeping through the haze of morning. The wind was blowing steadily from the south and Daniel estimated they'd reach port by early evening. His mind was focused on the task at hand. He'd discussed with Peter their options, once docked within the harbor.

Throughout the day he'd informed the crewmen their duty. There would be a definite reckoning between the two captains.

Daniel had never felt the rush of blood lust before, but now with the fire of his rage building in his blood he looked forward to the release of pressure that would come from the death of Cap'n Lefty Shakes.

He knew the man was old, but he had no excuse for stealing Brianna and Patty as he had. At least not that Daniel knew of. His eyes yearned to see Brianna and to know that she was indeed alive and well. His promise to keep her safe, to love her, and to cherish her haunted his mind. He felt guilty for having not been around when she'd needed him. The *if only's* ran rampant within his skull. If only he'd been close by when those men took them. If only he'd never let her go into town in the first place.

His worries were interrupted by the approach of Peter.

"You look terrible, Daniel. Have you rested at all?"

"No, I've been too wound up. I couldn't imagine resting. My nerves are edgy and my mind plagues me."

His kind eyes took in his friend's disgruntled appearance. "You'll need some sort of rest. We don't need you to faint away from exhaustion when we reach Tortuga."

"You're right. I know. It's just hard not to worry."

"If you dwell too much, you'll go crazy."

Daniel revealed a wry grin and said, "I'm afraid I'm already there."

Peter had to admit that Daniel's slight attempt at humor was a good sign. The plan for Tortuga was already honed to perfection. Each man only waited for the sign of the dreaded island. Peter knew that a rest was exactly what Daniel needed.

"Go to your cabin, my friend, and lie down for a bit. I'll awake you at the first sign of port."

"I'll go, but I'm not sure I'll rest."

He then turned and walked doggedly toward his quarters. Once there he plopped down on the edge of the bed and fell back into the soft comfort. His mind still raced, but soon his body eased and sleep claimed him.

Hours later Peter knocked on the cabin door. A refreshed captain greeted him.

"I had no idea how tired I was."

Peter just smiled.

"Once my head hit the pillow, I was out."

"I'm glad and we've just sited Tortuga. We should be there in thirty minutes or so."

"Wonderful," Daniel said, stepping into the sunshine. "Once we dock, I'll head ashore. Inform Wally that you'll be accompanying me. He and Tommy know their jobs."

"Yes, of course Captain," Peter replied, pleased at Daniel's rested composure.

Patty awoke in a strange uncomfortable position. What a hard lumpy mattress. She could have sworn the bed had been more comfortable the day before. She could hear rain falling outside and the occasional roll of thunder booming in the background.

At that moment a flash of lightening illuminated

the room. She wasn't in the home of Blue Eyed Charlie anymore.

The crude dwelling boasted a leaking roof. Her bed was pushed into a corner, which luckily didn't have any of the holes. The room was small and over to the far side sat two forms at a wobbly table.

"When do you want to enjoy the lady?" she recognized the voice of the greasy man named Slick.

"Oh whenever she awakes. I'll have to explain her new situation and all."

"Yes, that'll be interesting. Mrs. High and Mighty won't like it none."

"No matter now. She's here with us and we'll do as we like," said Rawlings. "She'll get used to it one way or the other."

Patty's nose started twitching. If she sneezed she knew the slimy toads would know she was awake. The tickle continued and finally she could fight it no longer.

A loud *aw chew* was heard throughout the shack.

"Oh looky, Rawlings, she's awake now."

"Afternoon, my pretty dumpling, you sure did sleep well."

The light of the single candle relieved the total darkness of the interior.

"We've got quite a mean storm raging outside and me and Slick's got a torrent to release inside."

Patty's mind froze. How did these evil men abduct her? She remembered talking with Brianna and then falling asleep. She must have slept hours.

"We wondered if you was ever gonna wake up," said Slick as he stood and moved towards her pallet. "You sure is pretty, light as a feather too."

"Yes, she's a delicate thing, Slick. We'll have to be careful. Don't want to ruin our toy too early."

"Yes, indeed," said the lard encrusted man. Patty's panic-filled eyes rolled over both men, Rawlings sitting casually by the table and Slick walking towards the corroded fireplace to add some more wood. Her size was barely half that of the giant man, Rawlings. Slick was shorter, but made of stocky muscle.

There'd be no possible way for her to overpower them. Besides, if she did she had no idea where she was. She could be anywhere on this stupid island. Her best bet was to bide her time.

Ah chew, she sneezed again.

The damp building wasn't helping her nose. She felt a burning row of welts on her upper arm. Mosquitoes had made a colorful buffet of the uncovered area. It itched dreadfully.

Scratching the offending spot, she sat up. A sudden wave of dizziness took her vision and she eased herself back down onto the lumpy pallet.

"I hope your not getting sick, love," Rawlings remarked. "These tropical climates are good at causing sickness."

Ah chew, responded Patty's twitching nose.

"Ah great, she's still sneezing, you don't reckon we snatched a puny one do you Rawlings?"

"She was well enough yesterday. Besides a head-cold won't stop me from trying the goods she has to offer."

Patty's nose and itchy skin caused her to be miserable and knowing that her ailments wouldn't stop the fumbling advances of her captors made it much worse. Her mind felt

cloudy and her forehead burned. She hoped she'd not con-
tracted a fever.

"Hey Rawlings. She's sleeping again."

"Well, that's fine. Means she won't complain while we
enjoy ourselves. You'd think she'd drunk a bottle of rum and
passed out."

"Yeah, she's real quiet."

Patty's almost delirious state saved her from the knowledge of what the fiends204 had in mind for her body. She
had terrible nightmares about goblins torturing her skin
with hot pokers. The flesh burned and in her mind she
could hear the sizzle of the tissues. The goblins laughed in
demented joy.

"She may be pretty, but she's not much fun."

The phrase barely penetrated her fevered mind. Slick and
Rawlings were disappointed in the response that Patty had
shown. It was at that point that Slick had brushed her cheek.

"Uh, Rawlings?"

"Yes, Slick, what is it? You sure are talking too much."

"Sorry Rawlings, but she's burning with fever."

"Fever?"

"Yes, her skin's all clammy and it's burning hot."

Rawlings had an acute fear of fevers. His parents had
both died from fever. They'd had weird colored spots and
the spots had oozed nasty puss.

"Oh great," he shouted. "I've got to go wash."

Slick glanced at his buddy in confused candor. "What's
wrong? You never bathe."

"It's the only way to keep from catching it." Slick sensed

the fear that now consumed Rawlings. "I'll not die of fever! If only we'd known she were sick before we touched her!"

"Rawlings?"

"Yes, what now?" He said as he rummaged through their meager belongings looking for soap.

"She's got some strange bumps on her arm."

"I'm out of here! Slick, you collect our things. I'm going to wash. Meet me at Pauly's Tavern in town."

"What about the woman?"

"Forget her. I've seen fevers like this. We'll all be dead before long. I plan on living."

"Alright then, I'll meet you at Pauly's."

Rawlings wasted no time cleaning his chilled body. The rain helped. The soap scrubbed his skin to a rosy pink as he rubbed the hard lye over his body.

Slick felt bad about leaving the helpless woman alone. His thoughtfulness didn't reach too far though. He stocked the fire up good and left the shack. He worried about the fever, but didn't have the fear like Rawlings. Fevers were just a part of life, after all. Funny how the strongest people often had the silliest weaknesses.

Rodrigo Diaz moved stealthily throughout Tortuga. He'd lived in this area all his life. Blue Eyed Charlie had been a good employer for some time now.

Rodrigo thought well of himself. The man Rawlings had made him look stupid. He admitted that the man had thoroughly taken him in. He'd thought the man was another simple pirate. The theft of Charlie's slave had happened right under his nose.

It made him look like a total idiot. He still wondered why he'd not asked the culprits what was in the bundle they'd toted out. He'd figured it was supplies or something, not one of the lovely slaves the trader made so much money on.

His task was simple; retrieve the lady before the men damaged the worth of the slave. A used slave was almost worthless, especially if the looks were affected.

Rodrigo had picked the trail up easily and a handful of witnesses remembered seeing the two men, one big and tall, and the other, stocky with slicked back slimy hair. They'd traveled the western road toward the abandoned shacks on the coast. He could smell the hint of smoke in the air.

If the storm let up he'd be able to see ahead better. The smell of the smoke got stronger and the shadow of the first shack came into view.

He could make out recent tracks in the mud around the door. Two sets had left this vicinity not long ago. Stepping inside he surveyed the rotted interior.

A stump of a candle sat burning on the table giving off enough light for him to see a bundle lying heaped in one corner.

Ah chew, said the bundle.

Rodrigo pulled the rag that was being used for cover back and discovered the woman he was searching for. He reached to shake her and felt the moan that eased from her parched lips.

The poor woman was burning up. He quickly gathered her up in his arms noticing how light she was.

Blue Eyed Charlie would be livid. It would please him to no end to find the scum who had taken the woman, but his first priority was the delivering of this sickly lady back to the hands of those who could help her.

He knew Molly would be waiting and ready to do her best to care for the woman. Trudging along in the light rain he wondered how heartless those cowards were.

Women were known to be the weaker sex.

That was one of the reasons he enjoyed working for Blue Eyed Charlie. He knew the man only dealt with men who could take care of such beautiful treasures.

All in all, the misuse of such a lady was such a waste.

Brianna's thoughts were interrupted by a commotion from the door. As the door swung in, a man carrying a large bundle and Molly came in.

"Sit her down over here, Rodrigo. I'll take care of things from now on."

"Yes, Molly."

The woman was eased onto the other bed and Brianna discovered that it was Patty.

"Is she alright, Molly?"

"I don't know, lovey. I've got to get these wet things off of her and take a better look."

"I'll help," Brianna said moving with sure steps to Molly's side.

The welts on Patty's arm were swollen and oozing. There were scratch marks where she'd been trying to relieve the itch. Her lips were cracked and there were bruises along her hips.

"Looks like the knaves used her even though she was in this state. Poor duck, probably didn't know anything was going on. There's a blessing in small things like that."

Brianna knew Patty's fear of rape had been a reality. She

just hoped Molly was right and that Patty had not been aware.

"What do you think?" Brianna asked after Patty had been washed and dressed in a soft nightgown.

"It doesn't look good. I'm afraid it might be malaria."

"Will she get better?"

"I wish I knew for sure. Sometimes people do and have bouts of the fever for the rest of their lives and then again sometimes they die. It's too early to tell."

Knowing the best they could do for her was to bath her in cool water and keep her comfortable the women settled in for a long wait.

""Stedey?" moaned Patty. "Stedey, where are you?"

Brianna's heart reached out to her friend. She, too, wondered where their husbands were and if they'd arrive in time to save them.

Ackmed Mohamed arrived at the house of Blue Eyed Charlie that afternoon.

"My good friend, I'm sorry to inform you that I will be leaving tomorrow morning."

"I am sorry to hear that, Ackmed," replied Charlie. "Will you be taking your blonde with you?"

"Yes, of course. I've already prepared her cabin. How is the other lady?"

Knowing his faithful guard Rodrigo had returned said lady; he now felt no remorse at informing Ackmed of her continued illness.

"Well that's just as well, my friend. I'm sure you'll find a good buyer for her."

"Yes, once she's on her feet again I'm sure it'll be no problem."

Ackmed paced the floor, "I'm not trying to rush you, but I am in a bit of a hurry. Would it be possible to fetch my slave now so I may be on my way."

"Yes, I'll send Molly for her now. It's a pity you can't stay for dinner."

"Indeed it is. Your cook is an artist. Such meals will not be frequent upon the sea."

A companionable silence fell as the men awaited the arrival of Molly with Brianna.

Then the women arrived and both men rose and shook hands.

"Be careful on your journey, Ackmed. The sea can be a vicious mistress."

"And you, my friend. I wish you luck in your trade."

He took the wrist of Brianna and led her away.

She was only now realizing that she'd be leaving her ill friend. Patty hadn't recovered much and if Brianna were being honest, she'd admit that the kind lady had worsened. Molly as was customary with her nature had not explained where she'd been called to. She'd assumed Blue Eyed Charlie had wanted to see her.

When she spied Ackmed Mohamed, she'd known her fate was sealed. She'd not meant to go along like a docile child, but at the sight of the tall and dark Turk she'd thought better than to challenge such a man.

They climbed into a carriage and drove toward the wharf. She could see the ships swaying on their moorings.

People ran to and fro, loading cargo and unloading the newly arrived ships.

One ship, which looked vaguely familiar, was arriving.

The carriage came to a stop at a large vessel. The name was in some foreign language she didn't know. As she stepped out and was helped quickly up the gangplank of the Turkish trader, she caught a glimpse of the name on the docking ship. It was *Enchantress*! Daniel was here!

That thought renewed her courage and gave her the added strength she needed to remain in her obedient state. She'd stay safe and remain quiet and then when Daniel came she'd be in good shape to escape.

The Turk led her across the dock to a small cabin at the end. The door opened and she was shown into a plush room. Trunks and pillows were scattered about in the typical Arabian style.

"Pretty Brianna, you will be most comfortable here. If you require anything else, please let me know. I'll be shutting you in until we leave, but don't worry, my flower, you will be freed soon."

The man's eloquent speech almost caused Brianna to fall into a fit of the giggles. Such decorative words were almost what one would expect from a Middle Eastern man. He looked to be trying to put her at ease.

Knowing that Daniel was here and would eventually trace the trail from the home of Blue Eyed Charlie to this vessel made her feel less chagrined toward this white slaver.

Daniel and Peter noticed the Turkish trader preparing to

leave. Neither paid it much mind as their thoughts were centered somewhere on the pirate infested island.

Once the ship was secure, both men were over the side and striding up dock towards the many taverns. They noticed the floating ship *Black Bird* that appeared empty. Evidently the crew hadn't felt it that important to stick around.

The crowd swarmed like blind hornets using their antennae to navigate the wharf. Men bumped into each other some polite, some not and quite drunk. It was a challenge to retain possession of their money and weapons.

A tavern ahead looked like a safe haven from the onslaught of the busy harbor. Walking inside, the two ordered rum and reached a private table near the back.

"Welcome, gents," said a heavily painted wench bending over the table to show her cleavage. "What can I do you for?"

"Nothing as of now," said Peter, "but if you can tell me where old Cap'n Lefty Shakes is staying, I'll throw in a nice gold piece."

"Will you then?" she said eying the handsome man up and down. "That's easy enough. The old scoundrel is not liked much, but he's upon the hill sponging off Mr. Blue Eyed Charlie."

"Really? Do you happen to know if he arrived alone?"

Giving Peter what was supposed to be a *come hither* look she said, "He had two ugly one's with 'em, which had large potato sacks over their backs."

Peter gave Daniel a wink and leaned over to deposit the gold piece in the valley of the lady's cleavage.

"Thank you kindly my lovely lady. Would you mind giving my friend and I some private time?"

"Not at all, sir. Not at all," she said, moving around their table and being sure to rub upon Peter's shoulder with her hands.

"You boys just call if you need anything."

Daniel couldn't help laughing after the lady had left, "Peter you are terrible."

"Whatever works, my friend. These looks I have are often handy when looking for information."

"I can see that. I almost thought you were serious."

"Not a bit. I should have been an actor."

"You're too good to waste upon the stage."

"I have to agree," Peter grinned. "I much prefer life on the sea."

SIXTEEN

Daniel and Peter left the tavern soon after. Their steps led the way to the home of the man, Blue Eyed Charlie.

"Afternoon governor, can I help you?" asked a tired Molly.

"Yes," answered Daniel. "I'm looking for a man named Lefty Shakes. I heard he was staying here."

"Indeed he is and if you'll step inside, I'll fetch him for you."

Following the now rejuvenated Molly; the men were situated in a comfortable sitting room.

Molly left the two and informed Blue Eyed Charlie of their arrival then headed in to inform the obnoxious Captain that he had guests.

This is what Lefty had wanted the protection from. Charlie wasn't worried in the least. He had only sold a slave who he'd been told wasn't attached to anyone. Lefty had brought him the women for profit. He knew nothing of their backgrounds. The other woman was sickly anyways. He'd gladly let them take her off his hands. Molly had told him that she thought it was malaria. Which would cause terrible repercussions if he sold her to anyone. His slaves were healthy not sickly. If anything, it would be quality control. Any businessman knew that you had to cut your losses at times.

Blue Eyed Charlie met Lefty in the hallway on the way to see the visitors. Lefty had not been told who they were, but Charlie noted that the old pirate had strapped on his sword. Surely he didn't think he could best a man so much younger than he. This would prove interesting.

"Gentlemen, to what do we owe the pleasure of this visit? Blue Eyed Charlie asked.

"I'm here to see a man called Captain Lefty Shakes."

"That'd be me, son, and I've been waiting on this moment for years," Lefty barked drawing his weapon.

"Sir, I demand you release my wife and the wife of Mr. Stede Bonnet."

"I don't take kindly to whelps who speak so boldly and besides I've not got your wife!" Lefty proceeded to take a fighting stance. "You'll die like your father did. I don't make idle promises and I promised myself the day I saw you sauntering through Bridgetown without a care that I'd finish the job I started so long ago!"

"Old man, I've had enough of your babbling, I suggest you explain yourself."

By this time Daniel had also drawn forth his sword. He'd not chance this crazy old man stabbing him before he got to Brianna.

Peter had also pulled out a blade. He casually waved it in the direction of Blue Eyed Charlie, but the man didn't pay him any mind. He was too intent on the drama at hand.

"I remember the day I gutted your father John Hammock. A fine day it was and your mother went easily also. The men saw to that," Lefty said, continuing his favorite rant. The years of telling had filled his brain full of extra nasty details.

"After she died and your dumb father threw you overboard, I had to send him to his grave, but not before he'd sliced the life out of my lower half." With this he used one of his hands to lift the edge of his shirt where a long mean looking scar covered his lower region. "I'll make you pay for what your father did."

Suddenly thousands of memories flew into Daniels head. He could now remember that day. The smell of the smoke as the other pirates pillaged the ship. He remembered the screams of his mother as she fought on valiantly until it was too late. He remembered his father's harsh voice telling Lefty that he'd gone too far this time. He remembered Lefty's evil laugh as he forced his father backwards against the wall of the cabins.

All the details that'd been missing for so long were now solid and this monster had not only killed both his parents, but also now threatened his life with Brianna. He wouldn't live to see the day finished!

"I do remember you! You caused many people to suffer, but I repeat, what have you done with my wife?"

"Ah, now boy, don't get worked up yet," he said shifting his weight from one foot to the other. "You should be pleased to know that my friend Blue Eyed Charlie over there," he said pointing in the direction of Charlie, "sold your lovely bride to a Turkish slaver this very day. In fact, she should be out to sea by now."

Daniel glanced in the direction of the slave trader in time to see Peter's face turn white. Anger blazed in his depths and the man named Charlie backed up in response.

"You know what kind of scum I hate most?" Peter asked Charlie.

"No, son, I have no clue."

"Well, I'll tell you," he said slowly closing the distance between them like a stalking cat. "Slavers!"

With that shout Peter lunged forward. Lefty dove at Daniel who fended off the dancing blade. To the unlucky end of Blue Eyed Charlie, Peter thrust his blade through the man's heart.

"You'll not sell another life! I'll make sure of it," and with a sharp twist he killed the distinguished, highly renowned Blue Eyed Charlie.

Lefty had ignored his friend's plight. Everyone died sooner or later. Today just happened to be sooner than Charlie had planned upon.

Daniel's pent up anger had given him a sixth sense.

Lefty Shakes moved about the room like a much younger man. You'd never have guessed that he was close to seventy.

Daniel was not going to let the madman go free. The sword thrusts began. Lefty would lunge. Daniel would swiftly dodge away. They both had eyes for each other, neither noticed when Peter exited the room to search the house.

"I'll kill you, old man!"

"You just try, son. Your daddy certainly wasn't a big enough man to kill me!"

Daniel contained the rage that surfaced anew at the taunts the jackal shouted.

"Come on boy, don't be such a pansy. Show me what you know."

Daniel sprung like a jaguar on fresh game, circling the man with the precision of a predator.

Lefty did a quick turn and slipped on the rug on the floor. Daniel's blade caught him in his upper forearm.

"You may have drawn blood, but I'll still see the end of you!"

In an insane attempt to catch his opponent off balance Lefty rushed the younger man not thinking on Daniels speedy reflexes. Leaping out of the path of the frothing gargoyle Daniel spun in time to see the odd mishap. Lefty hadn't figured on the large window by the door being open. Charlie had kept windows closed, but today being fresh and clear he'd thrown them open in hopes of airing out the stuffy room.

Lefty flew headlong into the open orifice and he grabbed at the sill in an attempt to save his spindly frame from falling.

Before Daniel could reach the edge he saw the tips of Lefty's fingers curl in cramped discomfort and crumple under weight of his used-up body.

Therefore, it was with no loss of pleasure, that Lefty's screaming descent onto the brick patio below was not with some ounce of justice.

Daniel hadn't killed that fool after all. His own obsessed temperament had done him in.

Surveying the room his gaze locked on the corpse of the dead slaver. He didn't think the world would miss him over-much. His eyes jerked towards the door as Peter reentered the room.

"I've found Mrs. Bonnet, Daniel. She's in a bad way."

Peter's frowning countenance spoke volumes.

"Did you find anything out about, Brianna?" asked Daniel as they walked down the corridor.

"Yes, I talked to Molly, she's the lady who was in charge of taking care of both Brianna and Mrs. Bonnet. She said that Brianna was indeed sold this morning and the the Turkish ship we spied upon arrival was the one that held her." Peter's eyes held Daniel's. "As I said before though Mrs. Bonnet's still here, but she's not well."

At a strong looking door, Peter knocked and was bid to enter by the diligent servant.

"I've done my best, sirs, but the lady's still suffering," Molly commented.

She'd already heard the commotion in the sitting room and decided that she didn't owe either of the dead men allegiance. Her many years under the strict supervision of Blue Eyed Charlie were finally over.

"How long has she been ill?" Daniel asked, taking in the lady's parchment skin.

"I'm not for certain. The two scoundrels who worked for Cap'n Lefty Shakes abducted her and she was sickened sometime then. Rodrigo, the head guard, retrieved the poor love," Molly said caressing the lady's brow. "Her fever comes and goes and her mind's fighting awful hard. Her symptoms haven't worsened nor gotten better. She keeps moaning for a man named Stede. I'm guessin' that'd be her husband?"

"He's even now on his way here. Peter, can you send for Wally and some of the other men? We'll see if we can move Mrs. Bonnet on board for comfort. Molly, you're welcome to come along if you like."

Peter nodded and left the stuffiness of the sick room. He'd seen Mrs. Bonnet in her prime and it saddened him to see the loss of such a vivacious spirit. Hopefully she'd recover.

Molly wrung a damp rag in a bowl and continued to bathe down Patty's burning skin.

"I'll gladly go along. I've had enough of this contaminated island," she said continuing her chore. "Your Brianna is a lovely girl. She's in good spirits, too. She'd mentioned that she knew you'd be along for her."

"Do you know anything about the Turkish trader who bought her?"

"Ackmed Mohamed is his name. He's been dealing with ole Charlie for years."

"And his ship left this morning?"

"Yes and he appeared to be in a hurry. Them Turks always are when there's good money to be made. He considered Brianna a treasure. Said she'd bring a fortune." Molly's hands stilled and eyed Daniel with a dissembling look. "If you hurried and we got this lady aboard soon, it'd be possible to catch him afore he got to far away."

"My thoughts exactly. If you'll excuse me I'll go arrange for the disposal of the bodies."

"Just tell Rodrigo that you spoke to SlapJack Molly and to take care of the mess. He should be near the kitchens."

"He'll not raise eyebrows at the order?"

"No, we've both been sick at this trading life. As long as he knows I sent ye, he'll go right along and if not, send him to me."

"Sure then," he said leaving the room.

Molly's eyes watched him depart. That man had suffered greatly over these years. He'd grown up nicely, considering the bad luck he'd had. Men were strange things. Some would grow bitter over such bad dealings, while others like the man who'd just left, would grow in strength and character.

Brianna sat confined in her chamber. Her treatment so far had been good. She couldn't complain about anything. In fact, her every wish had been catered to. Other than her release, of course.

She'd enjoyed a lovely dinner knowing she'd need the energy when Daniel arrived. They'd even supplied her with a couple books to read in order to pass the time.

Ackmed Mohamed had been pleased to know that his captive was learned. That further upped her value. His mind tallied the figures he'd received on the redhead last year. If his expectations could be met he would earn almost double on the sell of his new lovely.

The books hadn't held her interest long before her thoughts again settled on Daniel. Knowing that he was so close by helped ease some of her fear. She knew Daniel was capable and intelligent. It'd be only a matter of time before her hero saved her.

She'd learned one good lesson. Wishes shouldn't be taken lightly. Her life now was good proof of that. She didn't regret how things had turned out. Life was now exciting. Things happened that would normally have been the works of storytellers.

Her days of captivity had been full of wondering on what she should do and how she should act. Almost like when she'd lived in 2007 and watched movies or read books putting her in the place of the lead characters. Now she found herself recalling the different plots and learning from the mistakes she'd noticed them making.

The men onboard this ship, were all from the Middle Eastern area. They didn't speak English and she had a feeling that even if they did they wouldn't converse with her. The only man aboard who did was Ackmed Mohamed. He presented himself as a professional. All business and profit and reminded her of a Wall Street executive focused on buying and selling his high-priced stocks. She could almost hear the money being counted when he looked at her.

She had pocketed the knife that had been on her dinner tray. It amazed her that the trader and crew were so conceited in their ability to keep her aboard safely. She guessed they didn't expect her to fight back considering she was on a ship full of unknown people.

They even acted as if they had no fear of being absconded. She figured that Blue Eyed Charlie must have left out the fact that she had a husband who would be searching for her.

It was incontrovertible that Daniel would come for her, especially when she'd seen his ship floating in the harbor at Tortuga. She was glad that she wasn't on the receiving end of his wrath. She almost felt sorry for Cap'n Lefty Shakes—almost. He deserved whatever happened to his crafty hide.

Peter had told Wally to get a handful of men and follow him back to the home on the hill. He'd not told him anything concerning Brianna. He knew only that the wife of Mr. Stede Bonnet had been found and that she wasn't well.

The men Wally had chosen were careful one's. He knew

they'd do their best not to jar the lady as she was carried aboard the ship.

He'd discovered a feisty older woman in the chamber where Mrs. Bonnet had been staying. She had lost some fingers, was wrinkled, and stooped with the years of servitude on her, but her eyes were lively and knowledgeable.

He knew the woman, who quickly identified herself as Molly, would have been giving the ill lady the best care. He could tell she was rough around the edges, but deep down a kind woman tired of the craziness of pirate life.

Once informed that she would be traveling with them onboard in their search for Brianna, he felt an odd stirring of pleasure. It'd been so long since he'd talked to anyone other than the crewmembers. Molly could be close to his age and they could enjoy reminiscing about past adventures. He reminded himself that he was too old for romantic nonsense.

Molly was also pleased to find someone close to her age. It'd be nice to talk to a man who didn't act like she was a shriveled up prune. She still felt things. Even though her body was wearing out on her, she knew her mind was as sharp as any blade.

With the last of their cargo loaded, and the sickly Patty Bonnet ensconced in the captain's cabin with Molly close by, *Enchantress* set sail in pursuit of the Turkish ship.

Captain Daniel Storme prowled the deck. He wasn't looking for anything in particular, but going over the events of the day. His memories were now full of happy childhood days and loving parents.

The death of Captain Lefty Shakes had disappointed

him. He wished he could have been the one to silence the hate he'd seen in the man's face.

The fall Lefty had taken had broken his neck. Daniel could only take joy in the thought that the crazy demon, which the old man had harbored, had died with him. He knew he'd have to forget the evilness the man had caused. Such bad things should be left in the past and learned from. Grudges shouldn't be held, especially when the man was now dead.

Daniel had discussed with Peter his rash move to kill the slave trader Blue Eyed Charlie. Peter had said he felt driven to rid the world of that man. Peter had said he'd also searched the man's study and found thousands of records of women and children the man had sold. The world was well cleansed of those two.

From what Daniel could learn the Turkish ship was headed toward the Atlantic and then the northern coast of Africa. It was a long trip to reach the Bosprus and Istanbul.

Daniel hoped to overtake the trader sooner than that, knowing they were only a half day behind the ship, he felt sure they'd see the ship by nightfall or early morning.

Patty's condition wasn't the best. She'd wake long enough to talk to Daniel for a few minutes. She was weak and had only drunk small amounts of water and broth. Her once cheery complexion was translucent and pale.

She'd asked about Stede, and Daniel had told her that he would be there soon. That had comforted her somehow, even though Daniel had no way of knowing for sure.

Molly had finally told Daniel that she feared Patty had acquired malaria. The tropics swarmed with mosquitoes and it was highly possible Molly was right.

He'd known some who'd died of the dreaded disease. Chills had wracked their bodies, followed by fevers. The continuous cycle of these symptoms and the body's own weakness often ended in death. He hoped not for Patty.

Knowing how Stede loved her the man responsible would be found. Stede wasn't someone who took things lightly.

A calm nice gentleman to be sure, but he could also be a bulldog if need be.

Daniel had taken the names of the two men who'd allowed Patty to reach this state. It'd been the same who'd kidnapped both ladies from Bridgetown. Rawlings and Slick.

He'd asked around using the men's names and giving descriptions, but none had admitted to seeing them.

Rodrigo Diaz had proved helpful in removing the distasteful evidence of the deaths. Daniel had assured the man that he'd be welcome on his crew, but the man had refused saying that he wanted to open an exclusive brothel on the island. He wanted to use the contacts found in Blue Eyed Charlie's desk to gather lovely women to use in his venture.

Daniel had smiled, but inside wondered about the idea. What was the difference between the white slave trader and what Rodrigo Diaz proposed to do? Using women to make money, either way, seemed low and cheap to Daniel. He was certainly glad to be out of that pirate stronghold.

SEVENTEEN

Enchantress hadn't been at sea long before a ship was sighted off the port bow. Daniel had rushed to pull his spyglass out and see its colors.

The ship was dark black with gold letters proclaiming her, *Revenge*. He signaled his men to slow speed as he'd recognized the man stationed near the wheel.

It was Major Stede Bonnet.

Daniel hated to slow his pursuit of the Turkish vessel, but Stede had a right to see his wife. Her condition might improve at the sight and sound of her beloved.

"Daniel, its good to see you," shouted Stede.

"And I you, sir. If you'll come aboard there's someone here who'd love to see you!"

At this positive proclamation Stede gladly boarded the opposite side.

"Did you find our girls, then?" he asked giving the younger man his hand and a smile.

"I've got Patty below, but that Captain Lefty fellow had

already sold my Brianna into slavery. We're on our way now to try and catch the Turkish ship she's being held on."

"Well, I'll not keep you long then," he said. "So how's my Patty doing?"

"I'm sad to say, Stede, that she's not well."

"Not well?" he asked as his brows closed together in a frown.

"Yes, I'm afraid she's quite ill. I'll tell you the complete story on the way down. It's best you know everything, so you're not shocked at her appearance."

Stede was understandably worried at these words. His sweet Patty must indeed be doing poorly for Daniel to forewarn him of her appearance.

Daniel kept their pass leisurely. He knew the story would take some time to tell, but the man had to know all. The events of the past two days poured forth. Stede was astonished to learn that Daniel's memories had been restored. The total ordeal was unbelievably dramatic. The planning and selling of his wife, and the ultimate challenge of getting at Daniel had destroyed the wasted man. When it came to the part of Rawlings and Slick his face flamed in anger. Now his darling wife lay fevered and often delirious.

"Stede, please try not to excite her, she's very weak."

"Of course, Daniel. You know I'd never do anything to endanger her further."

Daniel nodded and they both stepped into the captain's cabin.

Patty laid on an array of pillows, water sat nearby on a table, and Molly had pulled a chair close by. She sat dozing in her chair.

"Molly," Daniel quietly said.

She jerked awake to look in the Captain's direction, "this is Patty's husband, he just pulled alongside in his ship."

"I'm glad you're here now, sir. She's growing weaker. Her lucid moments are fewer." Molly shook her head in slow movements.

"I've done my best, but now all I can do is help her to relax."

Stede was indeed astonished. His once glowing Patty lay ashen and faded. Her cheeks had sunk in from lack of nourishment and her hair had lost its entire luster. She used to be healthy and pleasantly curved, but now her bones were terribly prominent.

"Oh, Patty, my love," murmured Stede as he moved to her side. He clasped her thin hand in his and sat down in the chair Molly had vacated.

"Let's give them some time alone, Molly." Daniel said gesturing to Molly, as he turned towards the door.

Stede didn't pay attention to them as they left. His heart was solely on the woman before him.

He sat that way, speaking softly to her of his love, and the things he'd done since he'd last seen her. Tears started slipping down his cheeks and a fury started to grow within him as he marked the changes upon her beloved features.

As he looked out the window after several minutes of pondering what he'd do to Rawlings and Slick he heard a muffled sound.

"Stede? Stede is that you? Is it really you?" Patty asked trying to clear away her sleepiness, "I've been waiting for you for so long now."

"Patty, my love, you've been sick. You've got to get well now."

"Oh Stede, my dear heart. I'm afraid it's too late for that now."

"Don't say that," said Stede truly disturbed now. "You've always been a fighter."

"Oh, not so much as I let on. I don't remember much of what happened. I had an itchy arm and then I felt hot and cold at the same time."

Daniel had told Stede that Molly and he were convinced that she'd been mosquito bitten while Rawlings and Slick had held her prisoner. He could only worry now at what other horrible things had happened to her. He vowed not to ask. To do so might endanger her fragility. She was so delicate, nestled in the pillows.

"I remember waking again back at Blue Eyed Charlie's and then Molly being so kind as to nurse me. She's certainly a dear."

"Yes, I know all that love, but what you've got to do now is get better so we can go home."

"I'm not sure I'll see our home again, Stedey. Things have started slowing down for me. Sometimes when I'm awake, things appear fuzzy, like there are little candles dancing around the room."

"Don't talk like that, dear," Stede said trying to control his rising panic.

"Stedey, you've got to listen to me," she said, holding his hand tight. "You've given me more in our marriage than most people receive in a lifetime. My heart is truly yours. After I'm gone I want you to be happy."

"Patience Bonnet, you're not going anywhere and I won't have you talking that way."

"You're such a sweet man," she said closing her eyes. "I will love you always."

Stede stared in silent misery as his only love took her last breath. She'd waited to see him before she passed. She had to assure him of her love.

His eyes burned as the tears began anew. Soon he was started to keen in his despair.

The sound carried out the cabin and onto the deck where Daniel, Peter, and Wally heard the mournful wail.

"I guess the poor lass is gone now," said a depressed Wally.

"Yes, Stede will be inconsolable. He loved her intensely."

"Poor man," said Peter.

They all stared out at the sea, the unending sea. Each man thought of someone they'd lost. The sounds of Stede's anguish continued for what felt like hours to the crew, but in fact was only one hour.

He'd poured his heart out to the spirit of the woman he'd loved. The pain was a raw salt-filled wound, and the knife that kept turning in his chest existed because Rawlings and Slick were still alive. It wasn't fair that such cold-hearted mongrels lived while he'd lost the life and companionship of such a magical woman.

He'd find them and exact his revenge. They'd suffer for the death of his love. He knew that Patty would want him to return home and live peacefully, but truthfully, he didn't feel it would be possible, not while those men ran around free and alive.

His mind was made up. He rose and left Patty's bedside. His first point of business would be to get Patty home and buried safely. Then he'd reload the ship and set out on his search for Rawlings and Slick. He'd not rest until they were dead. His life no longer mattered.

Daniel had spoken to Stede as he emerged from his wife's side. He'd expected a completely depressed person, but Stede's carriage presented a man with a purpose. He informed Daniel of his desire to take Patty home to rest and asked for assistance in moving her onboard *Revenge*. Then he explained his vendetta in detail.

Daniel ordered men to help move Patty and he tried to talk Stede out of his quest.

"My mind's made up, son. Those two cowards are just as responsible for her death as if they'd been in the room and stabbed her with a knife."

"I know Stede, but you shouldn't let that ruin your life."

"My life's already ruined. Without Patty I've no purpose," he said watching the preparations between the ships. "My purpose now is to find justice for those men. It's all I've got to live for."

Considering the circumstances Daniel understood. He'd have felt the same if it'd been Brianna. He admired Stede's control. The pain must be tearing at his insides, but he still knew he'd have to hold things together until his mission was completed.

It saddened him to see such a good respectable man go down the disreputable path of pirate, but as Stede had said it would be a means to an end.

After Patty's small body had been moved the men departed company and Daniel continued his search for Brianna. They'd lost five hours during the meeting with Stede.

Stede had assured him that he'd not do anything too rash, but Daniel knew that with such a love as he'd lost, the man's passions of hate would brew uncontrollably.

The days began to blur together for Brianna. She'd assumed things would have transpired more quickly than they had, but here she was.

It'd been almost a week since she'd spotted *Enchantress*. Worries ran crazily throughout her cabin. She'd wondered at Daniel's delay. She wasn't very knowledgeable about ship speeds and the paths they took.

Her isolation had only been interrupted by the occasional appearance of Ackmed Mohamed. He kept a steady check on her health and mental state. So far she only seemed to be suffering from the usual slave shock. In fact, her introspection was driving her mad.

She'd learned from Ackmed that their trip would take around a month. They'd been gone almost one week now and the close confines of her cabin were old. She'd counted the nails in the walls and on the ceiling, rearranged the pillows, and read books she'd been given, and stored the knives from her plates. She had five now, strategically placed throughout the room.

The knife plan really went no further. She just figured it'd be better to have some sort of weapon around in case of an attack on her person. With the world around her being a large vast ocean, it wasn't likely that she'd jeopardize her good treatment. What would be the point in punishing herself? It's not like she had anywhere to run to.

She began to grow frustrated that Daniel wouldn't come. That he'd just move on without her, but then she remembered all their special talks. The interested way he'd watch her as she explained some of her futuristic objects. His sweet masculine laughter as she retold the adventures of movies she'd seen and his total interest in her as a person. Not just a body.

Deep down she knew he'd come. There would be a logical reason for his absence. There had to be.

Meanwhile, she'd have to find something to occupy her time.

That afternoon she debated ways to approach the subject of her boredom to the trader. Her dinner came and she'd enjoyed the meal with her usual zest.

"Sir, if you would. I'd like to know where exactly we are going."

"Ah, your curiosity has finally arisen. I wondered how long your intellect would take before your mind grew restless," he settled himself onto a plush burgundy pillow, "I will satisfy your thoughts. We are headed towards the Mediterranean Sea and then Istanbul. The markets there cannot compare to any others in the world," he said with unabashed pride, "Luckily for you, my flower, you will not have to endure the commoners market. I know of a prince in the area who has been looking for a jewel such as you for quite some time. He will be pleased."

Brianna began hearing the money counters, again. His eyes even glowed with the prediction of success.

"You will be happy there," he said.

Wanting to pacify him to assure his cooperation she smiled and said, "I'm sure I will, but in the meantime, what am I to do for now? From what you've said our journey will take some time."

"I will supply you with some books on translation and whatever else you wish from my library. It's quite extensive and should give you some sort of entertainment. Also I shall take you on afternoon strolls. Your health need not suffer from lack of fresh air."

"Thank you, that's most thoughtful of you." Ackmed's face beamed at her kind remark.

"Yes, of course, my flower, think nothing of it. Your best interests are in my mind always."

"Will you allow me to view your library soon, so I can begin studying?"

"Wonderful idea! Let us go now, and tomorrow will see you full of knowledge and promise." Ackmed led the short way to his chamber.

Throughout the room were books and charts stacked and organized in larger handmade baskets. He'd not exaggerated when he'd said if was extensive.

"I've sorted the books into a system I use to catalog my findings," he said walking to a large filled shelf. "I'm a collector of oddities. Anything new is always good. Feel free to look around and pick as many as you like. As you said before, it's going to be a long journey still."

She began a slow look around. It astounded her his

interests: books on cooking, different species of insects, diagrams of mathematical equations, and histories of various countries.

"I often select older used books. Something about their age fascinates me," he said, as she'd picked up a well-worn copy of the Koran.

Soon she'd chosen a handful of different one's and he led her back to the awaiting plush secluded cave. There she'd wait in lonely comfort until the next phase of her life arrived.

The rest of the voyage passed by uneventfully. She'd read and read until she was sick to death of books.

Ackmed had proven to be a friendly enough companion. They'd had the promised afternoon strolls and even a few games of chess. He'd been pleased to know that she played.

Although she rarely won, the games stimulated her dulled senses. Her tactical mind flourished with these chances to test her skill.

One morning, which had started like every other in the past three-and-a-half weeks aboard ship, she felt the ship slow and sway differently. Looking out her only window she could just make out a large town of many colors. People in weird dresses with turbans on moved about like ants of a huge mound.

The change in scenery was definitely welcome. The bad part would be the end of her freedom. Somehow the loss of that important factor was depressing.

She hoped it wouldn't be as bad as she expected.

Once the ship docked and the unloading began, Ackmed appeared at the door.

"My flower, it is time to go ashore. Your future awaits," announced an excited Ackmed. He'd miss this special slave. She'd proven to be good company and would be an asset to any man's house.

"You must cover yourself correctly and then we shall go to my home."

A large cloth of black was produced and she was suddenly covered in the dark fabric, from head to toe. She felt like a ghost at Halloween. To bad she wouldn't be going trick-or-treating, it'd probably be more fun.

With her new garb in place she was taken outside where Ackmed had arranged for guards to escort her to his home.

She was ushered into a carriage followed by Ackmed and the guards. One was posted inside while the other two took positions outside. She could view the city from a small eyehole in her cloak.

It was a crowded place with busy business everywhere she looked. A fresh market passed by where oranges, apples, chickens, and a variety of vegetables could be seen. It truly was living history.

A message had been sent to the Prince Edirne in Izmir. He would send a representative to determine if Ackmed's slave fulfilled the qualifications that the prince was searching for. Her worthiness would quickly to established.

Ackmed's home was located in a successful part of the city. His assets were safely stored in a local Jewish bank and his home was modest.

The carriage slowed to a stop and Brianna was led into the secure hallway of Ackmed's domain. A servant was ordered to take Brianna to the slave quarters. There she was divested of her heavy robe and her other garments.

Other servants arrived and silently drew her a bath with steaming tubs of water. She was lowered in the soothing depths and scrubbed until she was pink. She felt like a new person afterwards.

Sweet smelling oils had been rubbed all over her cleansed skin. Lotions that smelled of fresh lavender were smoothed in to her tender feet. Her hair had been washed and brushed free of tangles. When they all left the room, Brianna was sitting in front of a fire while her hair dried.

With the continued pampering, she started to wonder if her slave experience might not be half bad.

Pashal Ali arrived at Ackmed's residence several hours later. The trader's message had fallen on joyous ears, for Pashal, who was currently out of favor with Prince Edirne. A beautiful new slave was just the thing to put him back in his royal excellences good graces. A woman of great beauty never failed to please the overindulged personage.

Pashal was announced into Ackmed's meeting room. The sparse furnishings only accentuated the beautiful features of the women who were led into the chamber to purchase. The pale colors heightened the colors and delicate femininity of the lovelies. Each buyer left highly pleased and enjoyed Ackmed's well-known hospitality while experiencing the trader's good selection.

Ackmed had informed Pashal in the message of an extra-special acquisition. Even now he waited politely, while engaging in the usual small talk.

Finally the formalities were out of the way and Pashal asked, "You said you had a special woman for me to view, my friend? I am truly blessed that you would honor me with the delight of seeing such a slave. Shall we begin the parade?"

"Pashal, I would be most pleased to begin the parade. I will leave it to you to notice the one I spoke of. She truly will stand out well."

Ackmed clapped his hands four times and servants appeared to clear the refreshments. A door opened to the left of a giant chair and several beauties were brought out.

EIGHTEEN

Brianna awoke from a short nap when a young girl shook her arm gently. The girl then motioned for her to follow and she pointed to a handful of clothing items.

Piece by piece the gossamer articles were fitted onto her body. Rich shades of blue and green were woven throughout the fabric of dark purple. Small bright beads tinkled around the hem and wrists.

Viewing herself in the mirror provided she felt like a princess from Arabian Knights.

She was taken to a room full of other ladies. They varied in skin tone and race. She wasn't given long to observe the others before a group of attendants arrived and lined them up. One by one they were herded through a curtained off door. She could hear the *ohhs* and *ahhhs* of someone on the other side and then a variety of fast uttered words. She was next in line and closed her eyes as her turn came. A firm shove from behind propelled her into a dull colored room.

Ackmed sat beside a short furious looking man whose eyes grew round at the sight of her and then a crooked toothed smile appeared. The creepy little fellow then expressed what Brianna felt was a large amount of happiness of Ackmed.

She could tell Ackmed was pleased. Not knowing what to do she stood rooted to the spot and watched the conversation.

As she followed the flowing vocal play, she noticed how the little hairy one used his hands to further explain his words. Ackmed's smile grew wider.

Finally knowing his transaction was all but finished, Ackmed turned to her.

"My dear flower, this is Pashal Ali, he is the representative for Prince Edirne of Izmir, and has consented to purchase you as a token to his beloved monarch."

Brianna glanced from one to the other and had the strong impression that she'd passed some sort of test. Ackmed's excessive pleasure over a sell could only be bad news.

This prince must be a nightmare if the condition of Pashal's joy was any example. The scars on the man's arms didn't look natural either. What could a man have done to deserve those? All her thoughts came to a stop when Ackmed clapped his hands again and a large man appeared.

"Saul, will see you safely to Pashal's carriage. It has been a pleasure knowing such a jewel as you. I wish you much happiness," said Ackmed as a goodbye.

"Nice to know you too," said Brianna as the giant man led her away.

"She is English, then?" asked Pashal.

"Yes, but from the Caribbean area. No worries from England or any other part of that region."

"Wonderful. She'll be a true treasure. The Prince will be overjoyed."

Ackmed had also noted the scars. Those had not been there the last time he'd met with Pashal. The man must've done something totally thoughtless. When you had a ruler such as Prince Edirne it would be easy to cause the man displeasure. He was not a beloved prince to most of his subjects.

Lucky for Ackmed he stayed out of the politics of Turkey. As long as his sovereigns were pleased he had no problems.

Pashal climbed into the carriage relieved. It was good he could speak English.

"I hope you are well," he said. "Ackmed is a good man."

"Yes, I am well. Will the drive take long to our location?" she asked.

"Not as long as most. About one hour."

She smiled. He may look like a bucktoothed buffoon, but he was nice enough.

"What is the prince like?"

"I will leave that for you to decide. Some would say he is kind and others would not. It is better for you to come to your own conclusions."

Brianna's mind absorbed this information. A tyrant, evidently, she'd have to continue her docile role. She often felt like giving these overbearing men a piece of her mind, but she still knew it would be foolish.

One look at Pashal's arms assured her that a back-talking woman would fair much worse.

The ride continued in silence while each passenger was lost in his or her own thoughts.

"Mr. Ali, would it bother you if I asked about your scars? They seem very unique," Brianna asked breaking the quiet.

"I do not mind, for it was my ignorance which led to them," he said, scratching lightly on the many healed lines. "I was overheard in the garden giving my opinion on Prince Edirne to a friend. The one who overheard us was a sly fox. He used the information to ingrain himself in the Prince's favor. Prince Edirne was kind enough to spare my simple life, and leave me these reminders to forget the idea of opinions."

"What exactly did you say?"

"Only that I disagreed with his treatment of the city people. I felt that he enjoyed far too much food while so many starved in the streets."

Her ideas on the prince now darkened considerably. Politics had never been her favorite topic, but she couldn't help feeling drawn to this subject.

"I'm sorry to pry so much, but how did they create such odd lines?" she asked as her curiosity got the better of her.

"Do not worry about your questions. It is better for you to know now and be careful at the palace." His eyes took a faraway expression. "I was taken to the garden where I'd been overheard and a small fire had been lit. There were several guards present, for they understood the pain would cause the body to jerk. Knives where produced with blades that had jagged formations. Each knife was then heated over the fire and applied to my skin." A flash of the pain and fear of that moment crossed his features. "The pain was torment. My mind blacked out for a while and I was awakened by one of the guards. He threw a bucket of water over my face."

Pashal continued his story. He went on to tell of the

warning, as this ritual was called, that led him know that future mistakes in palace etiquette would result in death. He explained some of the people within the prince's residence who enjoy seeing others suffer.

She listened quietly, nodded, and gave sympathetic responses. Evidently this trip had been a last chance at regaining his lost position. She gathered that he wasn't extremely pleased with his life and would gladly leave it if offered the chance.

With his narrative finished, Pashal felt the weight of returning to the place where he once felt at home. The decorative walls of the building closed in around his soul and he started to get a claustrophobic feeling.

Brianna saw Pashal's pallor fade and knew he was on the verge of a panic attack. It was funny to her how stress even made the people in this time sick to worry. It just proved how everything was relative.

"Mr. Ali?"

"Please, call me Pashal. We know enough now of each other to use our given names."

"Fine then, Pashal. What keeps you working at the palace?"

"Our land is very poor and I was lucky to achieve the position I did with Prince Erdine. He needed someone to find lovely women for his harem and I knew many people due to my father's business in trade."

"Yes, but why do you stay on? Aren't their other princes who need the same?"

" I have never left this area and doubt I'd be allowed too. The prince doesn't take people who leave his employ well. It'd be a sure death sentence."

Men here were obsessed with controlling other's lives. To kill others because they wanted to leave your employ was barbaric, but she reasoned this era didn't care much for the rights of others, especially the poor.

"Pashal, let's change the subject and I'll tell you about me."

He smiled his lopsided grin and nodded. This woman was indeed special. Ackmed had not lied. She listened and noted his displeasure changing the conversation to something less tiresome. She'd not even complained, acted afraid, or scorned his friendly manner. She began her story with her marriage to Daniel, and then her abduction and her eventual sell in Tortuga to Ackmed. She explained that Daniel was even now following her trail and her hopes of rescue.

"If he does find you here it will be a miracle if you can escape."

"I know, but Daniel will not give up easily. He's got a stubborn nature at times."

"His persistence will be blessed if it is to be."

"I've come to far to give up hope now. Until I'm given a completely negative assurance, I'll keep hoping."

Pashal became thoughtful after this statement. His mind ran rampant with interesting new conceptions on escape for them both. If he could find this lovely woman's husband in the city soon, then both might flee this horrible place.

Daniel and the crew of *Enchantress* arrived one day after Ackmed and the Turkish ship. The delay of Stede and Patty had set them enough behind that they'd not been able to catch the fast-paced vessel. They'd sighted it several times, far away on the horizon, but wind and rain and other natural conditions kept them at bay.

Now in harbor at Istanbul, Daniel and Peter disembarked to find the home of Ackmed Mohamed. They had prepared for a fight or verbal duel. Swords sharpened and ready both men looked forward to the confrontation.

The long voyage had worn their nerves taunt and tempers were just a breath away. The crew had understood their captain's scowls and moods. They to were extremely piqued at the disappearance of the sweet natured Brianna.

Peter located Ackmed's home by asking a local market. The man at the stall cackled in glee that such English men would travel such a distance for one woman. The humor was lost on the men, but they flipped a handful of gold coins on the table and walked away. The gold further increased the man's mirth and he then offered them rugs, lanterns, oils, anything for the extravagant English, but Daniel and Peter were now lost to his excited talk as they followed the stall owners directions away from the market.

Ackmed's name was boldly engraved at his address. A shiny plaque assured them of his residence.

They knocked on the door and were ushered at once into the sitting room. Ackmed appeared with a stunned expression on his features.

"Gentlemen, what do I owe your visit too? It's not often we have English in Istanbul.

"I'm here to find my wife. According to the records found in Blue Eyed Charlie's office and from a witness, we were under the impression that she would be here with you," replied a controlled Daniel. He noted that this man wasn't threatening or confrontational. He only looked confounded.

"Your wife wouldn't happen to be the beautiful flower, Brianna, would she?" asked Ackmed.

"Yes, that is my wife," Daniel almost shouted, but kept his voice controlled. "Is she still here or have you sold her too?"

Ackmed could tell his position was very precarious. One wrong move and these two men would carve out his liver.

"I am very sorry to inform you that yes I did sell your wife yesterday ... " at Daniel's dark frown he continued, "please know that I was told nothing of her having a husband. Blue Eyed Charlie knew I wouldn't accept married women. It causes many problems. I myself admit that I was taken in by your wife's beauty and did not ask if she was attached, nor did she say anything herself."

Daniel's eyes burned in anger. It was a good thing for Blue Eyed Charlie that Peter had killed him, for Daniel would enjoy choking him at this moment.

"Listen, my friends. Let me clear things up as best as I can. My situation in the dealing was quick. I only called upon a friend from Izmir who works for Prince Erdine. He arrived shortly after and was so stunned by her loveliness he purchased her and should have arrived back at the palace yesterday afternoon. Ackmed's hands worried with agitation. "I will give you directions to his palace. I'm sorry to say that is all I can do. Prince Erdine is a fierce man and I'll not cross such a prince."

Peter's lust for the death of slave traders burned fiercely in his soul. Ackmed could feel the hate flowing from the man. Daniel was highly vexed at him also but for other reasons. A man's trade in this side of the world varied greatly from what he was used to, but he'd not punish the man for a bungled transaction. He'd said himself that Blue Eyed Charlie hadn't informed him of Brianna's married state. Molly had explained this to Daniel also. She'd said that the ladies backgrounds had been kept quiet from the buyer's.

"Peter, I think we've heard enough," Daniel said. "Let's get back to the ship and sail for Izmir."

Peter's look was dark, but he nodded in agreement. It'd not work out well for them to cause unneeded trouble in Turkey. Better to accomplish their mission and leave as soon as possible. This land made his skin crawl. Probably the knowledge that Istanbul was such a haven for those in the slave trade.

Daniel had left Ackmed with a warning to check on a purchase before he did anything and Ackmed had readily agreed. Peter had happily told him that Blue Eyed Charlie had met with his own demise and that he better not show himself in the Caribbean sea again or the same might befall him.

Ackmed listened intently and decided the Caribbean would be far too risky in the future. He'd stay closer to home. His accounts were doing well here and he'd not suffer greatly over the loss of trip expenses.

Aboard ship again, Daniel consulted his charts and according to his calculations, Izmir was towards the south and wouldn't take long to find. They left Istanbul and felt better knowing they'd find Brianna there.

Daniel worried anew. He'd learned from the market man that Prince Erdine was a crazy man not fit to rule such a nice place. His people died from lack of food and disease and he cared not a whit.

Medina sat beside the lovely English-speaking girl. She herself was from Saudi-Arabia and named after one of the wondrous cities there. She'd learned several languages in her quest for knowledge. She'd gained much favor under the rule of the evil Prince Erdine for her beauty and knowledge. She'd also bore the man a handsome son. The first of his expansive harem, the many other concubines had delivered girls.

She'd quickly been elevated to the prince's first wife and become the envy of the others.

Over the years, Pashal and she had come to an understanding and they'd often discussed the mean nature of their ruler. In fact it was she whom Pashal had been talking with when they'd been overheard.

Pashal had not been upset when she told the evil prince that she'd been scolding him of his opinions. He understood that she needed to protect her position as head wife.

She'd also had to be careful in raising her son. She refused to let the boy grow as spoiled and fat as his father. One day the pig would die and her son would rule with a kind hand. He'd been taught early on that his father betrayed his subjects by overindulgence, cruelty, and lack of caring.

Although the boy was only nine, he proved his kindness on various occasions by playing with his many stepsisters. He was careful that they never come to harm and shared with all.

Medina was very pleased at his growth. He'd be an excellent ruler.

She'd been lucky with Pashal's help and had kept the harem full of lovely women, but was careful to rid herself of any who might challenge her station. Those women usually found themselves as gifts to the prince's many neighbors. The gifts of these women helped bribe the other regions. All knew Prince Erdine was a useless mean figure, but closed their eyes in hopes the fat man would eat himself to death. The women were pleasant boons.

When Brianna arrived Medina's worries had jumped out. On speaking with Pashal privately, she'd learned the full situation. Pashal had even hinted at an excellent scheme to help their starving city. He'd explained that he'd inform her when the time was ripe, but that the less she knew the better.

He'd left the palace soon after to visit their small harbor in hopes of seeing the ship *Enchantress*.

Pashal had arrived early that morning. He'd not expected a soon appearance of the ship, but to be sure he'd arrived early just the same.

He'd positioned himself at a grogshop he frequented during his many bouts with stress-induced depression. Being that he was a normal customer he wasn't given any attention. He didn't drink anything stronger than tea, but found the atmosphere of the place soothing.

Here, any man could pour out his sorrows. His hope was that soon his sorrows would improve beyond measure.

About mid-afternoon, Daniel sighted the harbor of Izmir. The trip had been uneventful and he was eager to learn news of his wife. A plan had been forming in his mind, but as of yet the way of putting it into action had eluded him.

The ship sailed into the area without any trouble and was soon docked for the second time that day.

A scraggly looking fellow with crooked teeth approached from below.

"Is there a Captain Daniel Storme aboard?" shouted the fellow.

"Yes, there is," shouted back Peter. "And who might you be?"

"My name is Pashal Ali and I bring tidings of the captain's wife."

Peter looked skeptically at the man, but motioned him aboard. Daniel would be pleased. Something about the man's brisk pace reassured Peter's mind. The determined stride showed a readiness for action that all upon the ship would be pleased start.

"Daniel, there's a Pashal Ali here. He says he has news of Brianna," said Peter entering the cabin.

Daniel had been consulting a book on Turkey, but closed the book and looked up with an expectant look.

"Captain Storme, I have much to tell you and we have much to accomplish," started the hairy tooth impaired man. "Your wife can be returned to you this night, but I will need your help on escaping this place."

Daniel nodded and waited for the man to continue. Pashal was pleased on meeting Daniel. The man appeared just as capable as Brianna had described. The plan would work. Many lives would be blessed from this expedition, including his own.

NINETEEN

Brianna sat with Medina awaiting the return of Pashal. Her carriage ride from Ackmed's had proved to be important. She'd made a good friend with the little man. He'd said he'd help them all.

Medina sat with her. The two had talked things over. Brianna had soon learned how strong the woman actually was.

She'd been raised to this harem life and was in her element.

It was now early afternoon and they'd become restless.

Medina had been careful and hadn't allowed Brianna access to the harem. As far as the others knew she did not exist. They'd not learn of her presence unless absolutely necessary.

An odd scratch at their chamber door brought Medina quietly to her feet. She cracked the door and soon opened it wide to admit a cloak-covered form.

Once completely in the room and the door closed the hood fell free.

Brianna gasped. Before her stood her beloved Daniel.

"How did you get here?" she asked in awe.

He smiled and responded, "Your little friend Pashal found me at the harbor. We've not got much time now. He's having an audience with the Prince for the last time." With that his eyes landed on Medina and he explained Pashal's part, "Even now your husband should be resting eternally."

Medina blinked in understanding. "He did appear tired today. It must have been the dinner last night." She smiled a secretive smile and looked at Brianna.

"You both must hurry. When he is discovered a cry will arise and I will not be able to help you if you are caught."

Daniel pulled a similar cloak from beneath his padded form. "Put this on and we'll be on our way."

"Thank you for everything, Princess Medina."

"Don't humble yourself my child, tell Pashal he has blessed us with our freedom and to return to us one day later on."

"I will."

The disguised figures crept out into the dim corridor down a winding flight of stairs and through a back garden gate.

A heavy laden wagon sat outside the gate. Rugs and fabrics were stacked in neat rolls. The cloaked duo climbed into the seats and clicked to the horses. The wagon wove a slow path through the afternoon crowds moving in the direction of a sleek merchant ship.

The load was parked close by and the figures started carrying the light weighted silks.

The whole affair was so commonplace that the people of the harbor went about their business.

Tomorrow would show the locals unable to identify

the merchant craft. So many ships came and went another would matter little.

Pashal was quickly accomplishing his many deeds. He had acquired an audience with Prince Erdine around his early dinner hour.

Prince Erdine truly enjoyed food and ate every two to three hours. Each meal was at least four courses and consumed with amazing gusto.

Pashal had sat quietly while the large monarch inhaled a fat pigeon, soaked in a cream sauce. The sauce, a yellowish liquid, oozed down the great one's face.

The bird's bones lay in wild disarray upon the large platter. His bloated lips smacked in relish.

"You requested an audience, Pashal. I'm still mad at you. Have you come bearing gifts?"

Pashal smiled a knowing smile. This whale of a man was so predictable. "Yea, my great prince, a lovely English rose with golden hair and green eyes." As he said this he reached over and carefully refilled the prince's glass. The small dose of poison dripped easily between his fingers. He handed the topped off drink to the awaiting grubby grip of the obese man.

"That pleases me, but I will truly know when I see the rose myself."

Prince Erdine downed the liquid and sat back savoring the chocolate confection still residing on his tray. The chocolate mousse soon met the pigeon in the man's stomach.

"She is a definite prize, my prince. Her mind is as lovely as her person."

The prince smiled as his eyelids dropped. His plump

hand fell with a plop to his side and then his head fell forward. Pashal was careful to leave the man as he'd died. The poison he'd used wouldn't be detectable by the standards here. He'd ordered it years ago from a place far away in Egypt not thinking he'd ever need it to kill the prince.

He eased his way down the many hallways and out the back entrance. Anyone seeing him would assume he was on an errand from the prince. The man's body wouldn't be noticed until they came to remove the remains of the meal. He had just the amount of time he needed to reach the safety of *Enchantress* in the harbor.

At first the poison wouldn't be detected. It would be days before the call was raised for his death. Medina would be careful in the next week. She'd rule discreetly behind her young son until he grew mature enough to take over.

The citizens of Izmir would not mourn their fat prince. They'd be to busy feasting from the food the palace would no longer need.

Pashal had donned a similar cloak to that of Brianna and Daniel. He pulled the hood lower over his eyes and walked amid the other people of the wharf.

The wagon full of rugs was still in the process of being unloaded. Each form carrying the many carpets wore cloaks, hoods hiding their features.

Pashal grabbed a burgundy-fringed rug and joined in the procession moving the freight to the ship. Once his feet met the deck he worked his way toward the captain's cabin.

Inside Daniel and Brianna had been talking. The main goal right now was to load their *cargo* and leave as soon as they were finished. The tension of the past month evaporated when they'd embraced in a long welcome kiss.

Pashal entered and said, "I'm sorry to interrupt, Captain Storme, but the cargo is almost on board."

"That's fine, Pashal. Did you succeed?"

"Yes, it is finished," was all he said.

Pashal, we've made you a cabin below decks if you'd like to go rest. I'm sure you'd feel better waking away from here."

"That is thoughtful of you. I will rest now."

Both had noticed Pashal's strained appearance. Leaving your home could be hard. The conditions for Pashal had been emotional. It took great strength of character to do what he had done. Murder wasn't something anyone took lightly, but often the need was there. Many would prosper under the new prince. One day, far away, the pain of the present would be forgotten.

The room assigned to the hairy man of Turkey was small including a short table and cot. As his eyes adjusted to the dim interior his anguish filled his soul.

There had been much more to the day than he'd explained to the captain and his wife.

His heart was full of misery at the leaving of his country. It wasn't his patriotism that pulled at the chords. It was the dark haired Arabian Princess Medina.

Many had speculated over Medina's ability to give Prince Erdine a son when all the other women had only birthed daughters. Pashal knew the truth.

Ten years ago, the magical Medina was given to Prince Erdine as a token from her father. The man had loved her dearly and had hoped that the Prince of Izmir would also. In a way it had happened. The prince was taken in by her beauty and intelligence, but it was the prince's servant, Pashal, who had loved her from the first.

Pashal had loved her from afar until one day she'd approached him. He'd known for sure that his body would repel her. Oddly enough after being in the evil prince's arms, Pashal Ali had looked like a handsome man.

She'd really been attracted by his kindness and his worry over the people of Izmir. Her upbringing had taught her that a compassionate man made the best ruler. Compassionate was something Prince Erdine was not.

The one night they'd spent together had resulted in the boy. That boy would now be Prince of Izmir.

Medina had never approached Pashal again except for conversation. She enjoyed his mind and had gotten what she'd been after.

It had been hard for Pashal to see his son growing up from a distance. He'd never gotten to love him as a normal father could. No hugs, no birthday surprises, or just seeing the knowledge brighten his eyes.

He was proud of the boy. Medina had been kind enough to tell of the child's exploits. First words, his schooling, his good-natured heart. All this warmed him; his son was now a prince.

One day he'd return, it would be a long wait, but worth it. The secret of the child's parentage would never be revealed. With his disappearance the succession would not be questioned. For the killer, if they ever noticed, would not be found. Besides many would overlook the death of such a man when the good of the new was discovered.

Brianna and Daniel sighed in relief as *Enchantress* left Turkey. They'd asked for privacy with no interruptions and the crew gladly agreed.

Captain Storme and his lady needed time to talk and cuddle.

It was almost the spring and they were once again together.

"Bri, I think you've gotten more beautiful while we've been apart."

"Don't talk nonsense, Daniel, my love. You just missed me," she said as they lay blissfully in each other's arms on the comfortable bed.

"It's not nonsense. You're a sight for my sore eyes. I'll not let you out of their gaze from now on."

His thoughts were just that. He'd take his wonderful wife and keep her close so she'd stay safe.

"Suits me fine," she said kissing his nose. "You have such nice eyes and being captured like that would be divine."

"So you're truly well after your long adventure?"

"Yes, I'm fine, really Daniel. Don't worry so about me. It was all exciting and I didn't suffer badly. It could have been much worse."

Daniel looked surprised for a moment and then felt compelled. He hated to bring sadness to their reunion, but she would find out eventually. Better now when he could hold her. "I do have some bad news to tell you. I've actually waited longer than I should have."

Brianna's eyes clouded with fear, "What is it, Daniel? Are you alright?"

"No, dear heart, I'm as healthy as an ox. It's about Patty."

Briannas mind blurred. How could she have been so selfish as to not ask about her friend? Patty had been so sick when she'd last seen her. So much had happened, but it disgusted her to think she'd not spared a moment to ask about her.

"Is she okay?"

"She is now," he said holding closer to ease the pain. "Remember I told you Stede caught up with us and delayed us by half a day."

"Yes."

"Well, he came aboard and went to sit beside Patty's bed. The poor woman was so sick. She'd been in and out of that fever. It'd pulled her down to nothing. Stede held her as she took her last breath. He was in such pain. She was such a good woman to die like that."

Brianna's eyes misted. The tears started to fall. Daniel held her close while the rush of despair claimed her. He couldn't help thinking how lucky he was to find a woman who could love so deeply. She'd been through much with Patty.

After a while her hiccups could be heard.

"I guess, I'll need to drink something before I dehydrate," she said. "Is Stede doing better?"

Daniel sighed, "No, I'm afraid he's let the hate get to him. He's sworn he'll find Rawlings and Slick and seek out his revenge."

"Patty wouldn't have wanted him to do that."

"Yes, but you see, with her gone now Stede said he had nothing to live for. Since he's alive and well it gives him a goal. Something to keep him going."

"I understand. It's just so sad to see such a love destroyed, and a little frightening."

"I'll keep you safe, love. Don't worry about that."

"I'm not worried at all," she said trying to be cheerful. "I know you'll do your best and so will I. We'll work out our lives together."

He kissed her forehead and then downward along her neck. She'd not lied when she'd said she missed him. This was one of the parts she'd missed most.

He was such a passionate man. When he released his fire it scorched her skin. Waves of hot lava moved in her veins and soon both loved like there was no tomorrow.

The long passage home would be a second honeymoon of sorts for the lovebirds learning the contours of each other's bodies and placing each freckle and curve to memory would be their aim.

TWENTY
one year later

1718, Bridgetown, Barbados

Daniel paced restlessly in the sitting room downstairs. A decanter of rum lay haphazardly on the table. His glass had been refilled countless times.

Again he heard a deep moan come from their upstairs bedroom. His scowl deepened.

"Daniel, you're going to wear a run in the carpet with all your walking back and forth, sit down," urged a patient Duncan. "The lass will do fine. You know that girl's made of stout stuff. She'll be through before long."

"I'm sure your right, Duncan, but that doesn't calm my nerves. Its just been going on too long."

"Its only been six hours, son. These things take time."

"I know, but I hate to hear her suffer."

Daniel reached for the bottle again just as a loud scream rent the air. The whole house was filled with the nerve-wracking sound. He ran to the stairs and was at the door in the blink of an eye.

Margaret's face peeped from the other side, "Mr. Daniel, go back downstairs, everything's fine here."

A large high-pitched wail accompanied her words followed by another.

"I'm not moving a muscle. I want to see my wife," he said pushing at the crack.

"Listen, I know you're the boss here, but she's not even cleaned up yet. She's tired, too!" said the stubborn Margaret.

"Margaret, please let him in, I miss him," said the weak Brianna.

"Fine, but don't you tire her none. She's had quite a time."

Daniel stepped inside as Margaret moved and peered at the bed. His wife lay propped up on some pillows, looking exhausted. Her sweat damp hair lay in strands down her face and she moved slowly in discomfort.

Two swaddled forms lay near her face and as he moved closer he noticed to two babies.

"My sweet husband," Brianna whispered, "meet your children, little Donal and tiny Brandi."

"Yes, and healthy ones at that," chimed in Margaret. "Your wife is a strong woman. She pushed both babes through in no time."

Daniel's hand reached out toward the closest baby. The little fist of the infant punched out in response.

"That's Donal, he's going to be a handful," said his loving mother.

Daniel's eyes moved to the next baby. It's little heart-shaped lips turned up at the corners in a hint of a smile.

"And that's our Brandi, she'll be a heartbreaker."

Twins. He'd never thought that he'd have two babies at once.

"You're amazing, Bri."

She smiled in response and closed her eyes. He leaned over to kiss her and could feel the love flowing around the room.

Margaret left the couple to their musings. She'd gathered up the soiled linens and cleaned as quietly as she could.

"There you are woman, what's going on up there?"

"Well, my noisy husband, the Captain's got two lovely babies now."

"Two?"

"Yes, twins dear."

"Well I'll be, is Mrs. Brianna doing well?"

"Good as can be under the circumstances."

"I'll say one thing, when Daniel does things up, he does'em right."

Margaret slapped his back and said, "Go on, you. I've these things to clean up," she said pointing to the linens, "You might as well go tell the others."

Duncan found Peter, Wally, and the scamp Tommy out back on the patio.

"Is Mrs. Brianna doing alright, Duncan?" asked a worried Tommy. "We heard the worst scream!"

"Oh, she's doin' right fine lad. She's done had Daniel two sweet babies."

Peter smiled, "I guess that's double-trouble for our Daniel."

"Indeed, one boy and one girl, and trouble from each no doubt," commented Duncan.

It was good to see Peter smile again thought Duncan. After the return from Turkey he'd taken a serious way of thinking. He'd only now began to unwind. He was much more himself these days.

"One day I'll have to find me a special lady like Daniel's Brianna." Peter said recalling how the two met.

"Doubtful that it'll be anytime soon," he said a little sadly.

"Son, don't worry. Someone's out there," Wally remarked trying to keep Peter from resuming his woeful tendencies.

"I know. It's just seeing the love between those two makes one long for the same."

Duncan nodded. He understood all too well about the magic of love. Margaret had consented to be his bride less than a year ago and he couldn't say he regretted the move.

Molly appeared at the steps of the patio carrying a large tray. She'd brought some lemonade for her boys, as she called them. It was funny, but SlapJack Molly had fit right into their odd household.

Wally and her had spawned a deep friendship. Both were too old for the romantical stuff, but the company couldn't be better.

Daniel appeared soon after. His eyes glowed in happiness.

"Son, you couldn't be looking more pleased." Duncan said grinning, "two youngin's at one blow."

"Yes, they're a surprise, but a welcome one."

"How's Mrs. Brianna, Daniel?" asked Wally.

"She's tired out and resting now. I don't know how she did it."

"Women's got inner strength," Molly said pouring Daniel a glass, "from the looks of your eyes you need some lemonade."

"I did consume quite a lot of rum."

"Worry'll do that to ye," Wally said winking.

"Especially when it's one you care about."

A dog began barking around the front of the house.

"Sounds like Tiny's up to something, again." Tommy said jumping down from his seat, "or maybe someone's here." He took off at a run around to the front of the house while the others looked on in amusement.

"You expectin' someone, Daniel?" asked Duncan.

"No, unless it's something important."

At this comment they all arose and followed Tommy's trail around the side of the house. A dark carriage had just come to a halt in front of the doors. A footman jumped down to assist a middle-aged gentleman from its depths.

"Well, I'll be snookered," said a grinning Wally. "It's Mr. Richard, himself."

It'd been almost one year and a half since Daniel had last seen his stepfather. They'd kept up with letters and such, but hadn't had time to visit. Now here he was looking well and on the day his children were born.

"Richard, it's good to see you," Daniel said pulling the man into a bear hug.

"It's been some time, son. You're looking fit. Where's that young bride I've yet to meet," inquired Richard Smithfield.

"She's resting upstairs."

"Nothing wrong with her or the babe I hope."

"Nothing of the sort, in fact she delivered twins just a couple of hours ago. Needless to say she's tired."

"Indeed, what a momentous occasion. Such a wonderful

welcome gift. I hope you don't mind me enjoying these new grandchildren."

"Not in the least," Daniel said knowing how Richard still considered him family even though they both knew the truth of his past.

"They'll be pleased to know they have such a doting grandfather."

"I'll probably spoil them dreadfully."

"You won't be the only one spoilin' them children," winked Wally.

"Wally, you old coot, your still moving around I see."

"Yes, Mr. Richard, I'd not let that Daniel go without me. 'Sides I've got me a companion now," he said pulling Molly's hand.

"Ah, yes. I guess this would be the famous SlapJack Molly. I've heard much about you my dear."

"None good, I'spose," she said.

"On the contrary, my dear, everything good. From my correspondence with Daniel I've learned you were a good help to my friend, Stede Bonnet's wife. I do thank you."

"Think nothin' on it sir. She were a good woman."

"Indeed. Well, Daniel, if you'll take us inside I'd like to get settled."

"Sure, Molly would you prepare a room for Richard? I'm going to tell Brianna of your arrival."

"Don't wake her on my account, son. She's had a big day and deserves her rest."

"I know, but if I didn't tell her you were here she'd be madder than a hornet at me. She's been wanting to meet you for quite some time."

Duncan and Wally went back to the patio and Daniel and Molly went inside. They could see Tommy and the nut Tiny wrestling near the stables.

Tiny had decided the cabin boy was fun and visited as mush as possible. Often the duo was seen splashing through the puddles and chasing hares in the fields.

The arrival of Richard had offered the pair a chance to frolic like young ducks. It'd rained the night before and big puddles could be seen on the other side of the stable. Before long their encrusted bodies would arrive at the kitchen for a snack and Margaret would scold them soundly, but for now they'd wallow like two slick pigs.

Brianna was up and about sooner than anyone expected. She'd rested for two days and now was itching to get up and about. She couldn't stand laying about when there were visitors around. Her babies lay peacefully in their cribs with a watchful Molly close.

She'd met Richard, finally. They'd gotten on famously. He'd regaled her with many stories from Daniel's past. She'd learned so much more about the man she loved.

At dinner one night he'd brought up some disturbing news about Stede. Evidently, he'd caught up with Rawlings and Slick from the help of the notorious Blackbeard. Unfortunate for him, Blackbeard had proved a tricky man. After being held hostage by the pirate, Stede had moved toward the coast of the Carolinas. Life looked slim for their friend.

"What are you thinking, love?" Daniel asked sneaking up behind her and putting his arms around her.

"Many things," she answered. "Mostly about how much I love you, I was also thinking about Stede."

Don't dwell on it much, love. He'll find Patty eventually."

"Yes, I know. I'm just afraid it'll be sooner than even he knows."

Daniel understood their friend had gone over the deep end. His revenge had been paid, but he couldn't give up the life of pirate. The excitement was all he lived for.

Daniel nipped at Brianna's earlobe.

"You're such a tease," she said. "Don't pick on me, you know we have to wait a couple more weeks."

"I know," he said. "But I couldn't resist such a tasty morsel. Do you regret our lives, dear heart?"

"No, my love, never! Regrets aren't possible when I've finally found a love like ours. You're my wish come true!"

AUTHORS NOTE

I hope you enjoyed Brianna's story. The characters I used were all fictional except Major Stede Bonnet.

Major Stede Bonnet was indeed a pirate from 1717–1718. The reasons for his turn to piracy are shrouded in mystery. I chose romance as a reason although accounts that he turned to piracy to escape a shrewish wife are out there. He did meet up with Blackbeard for a time and eventually died December 10th 1718 by hanging. An odd gentleman and pirate, for sure.

I'd love to hear from you, if you'd write:

mist_tempest@hotmail.com

423 Bradshaw Lane

Hiawassee, GA 30546

Best wishes to all:

Katherine Bower